HEATHER GRACE STEWART

Good Nights

Love Again Series
Volume Two

Good Nights
Love Again Series, Volume Two

By Heather Grace Stewart

Edited by Jennifer Bogart

ISBN: 978-1-988248-03-5
ISBN: 978-1-988248-02-8

Also by Heather Grace Stewart

http://author.to/hgstewart

The Ticket: Love Again Series, Volume One
(Also available in Audiobook)

The Friends I've Never Met

Remarkably Great

Strangely, Incredibly Good

Caged: New and Selected Poems

Dedication

for Bill and Kayla

for the thousands of good days and nights! xo

Thanks

Thanks to my dear family and friends. Your encouragement goes a long way in keeping me at my writing keyboard, even the seemingly small gestures like a little text emoticon with hearts or high-fives. Thanks to Natalie Marie, Dave Cenker and Ravendra Patel for being my first enthusiastic readers and commenters on Wattpad; to Jennifer Bogart, my friend and eagle-eyed editor, Morning Rain Publishing, and Lucy Rhodes at Render Compose for her brilliant cover design, and Mark Dawson and James Blatch of Self-Publishing Formula for your sheer brilliance and continued support.

Above all, thanks to my loyal readers of 20 years, and to my new ones. I couldn't do any of this without you.

One

Hannah

<I can't be married to you anymore. I'm sorry.>

I choke on my toasted sesame bagel as I read the text from my husband. Bending forward in my brown leather chair, I cough the bagel up into my other hand. A large chunk of undigested bread and cream cheese lands in my palm. Gross. Just how my insides feel right now. Gutted.

"Sorry, please continue," I say to my eight colleagues at the table, but it comes out raspy and uneven. I wipe my hand on a napkin. "Good ideas, people. Let's keep going. We need the excitement to build more than ever for this episode. What would Faith say in this situation? How is Ben going to react?"

The room grows noisy again as my writers begin throwing around ideas. I force myself to blink, then reread Doug's text. It had to be a joke. This didn't happen. Your husband of ten years doesn't just text you that he wants a divorce. Does he?

My right hand starts to tremble, so I place my cellphone on my knee under the table so no one will notice. Of course, my best friend, Jillian, does. She is astute even before her first cup of coffee.

"Psst," Jillian gently leans into me as she whispers, "what the hell is going on?"

I inhale to calm myself and rotate the phone so Jillian can see the text. Within seconds, Jill's intense brown eyes grow large. Her face reddens and contorts into anger.

Jill grabs the phone and quickly texts:

<Piece of crap! Always hated you>

I take the phone back and delete the text before it can be sent. Instead, I type:

<Can we talk about this?>

This feels so out of left field. Sure, we'd drifted apart in the last five years, but I thought we were rekindling our love. We'd talked about going to the South of France just last week. Or, at least, I had talked about it. We were sitting in the living room sipping red wine. That was rare for us, because, we both admitted, we'd been married to our jobs for far too long. The public knew us as Hannah Storm, successful television series creator, and Doug Evan, Broadway actor and producer. We wore whitened smiles for them, and when they shoved microphones in our faces on the red carpet, we told them we were brilliantly happy; couldn't be happier. In short, we lied. The alternative was too painful.

One night last year, Doug flew into a jealous rage, throwing magazines and papers across the bedroom. He'd had too much to drink, but jealous temper tantrums had always been part of his personality. That time, he was ranting that he'd spent the last six months flying from Vancouver to New York every week to be on Broadway, and despite good reviews, he hadn't been nominated for a Tony.

Meanwhile, my show, written and produced in Vancouver, had been up for an Emmy. Doug smashed our framed photos on the floor and started yelling all kinds of obscenities at me, saying we'd gotten lost in how others saw us and forgotten who we'd once been. He said he didn't think I even deserved the Emmy.

The next morning, he apologized for the outburst, and I somehow found it within myself to forgive him, but it was hard for me to forget. I lived in fear of him after that, but I had to hide my nervousness from my Mom, who was never fooled, and the public. It was not an easy mask to wear. That afternoon, we tried to remember the old Hannah and Doug. He seemed to want to make amends. We went to the movies and had lunch in a quiet café.

When I mentioned France, he'd quietly kept scrolling on his phone, not even looking up. I suppose I should have realized what that meant, but I thought perhaps he was just tired. He's been distant all year, and it seems he's spent more time in New York and LA than here with me. I always assumed he was preoccupied with advancing his career.

Over the last few months, my show has gained a large online following, but it's floundering in the all-important ratings. Doug hasn't said anything to lift my spirits. Not one surprise to say he misses spending time with me. Now, he's ending "Us," by text message.

I read his next message, blinking back the tears.

<You and I both know, it was always a starter marriage, H. You're getting divorce papers at the office today.>

Always a starter marriage? I feel the walls closing in on me, like inside a car wash, the pressure building in my head. We grew apart, but not once did I feel this was a trial marriage. I thought he was my one and only.

But what about Doug? Is there someone else, or has he simply fallen out of love? I close my eyes, and the room starts to spin. Ten years. A husband, a cat, and a sarcastic parrot. The beautiful house we built in Burnaby. We'd even talked about starting a family once our careers slowed down. I feel like I am standing at the top of a canyon, and everything I'd worked for this last decade is falling away from me, spiraling down into deep, dark crevices out of my reach. Everything is gone.

I open my eyes again and find everyone at the table staring at me, looking perplexed. I inhale deeply, put down the phone, then exhale, and attempt to put into words what I am feeling. I'd always been honest with this crew.

"My marriage is over. I don't want to talk about it. I need to put my energy elsewhere. We're going to write the best finale we can and pray we're picked up for a fifth season. I'll be in my office if anyone needs me. But..." I push back my chair and stand up, "give me a half-hour to process this, guys, okay?"

I feel Jill reach out and touch my arm. Trying to console me, I assume, but I pick up my pace. I just want to be alone. As I make my way down the corridor to my office, I hear my phone ping. I'd been late for dinner the last few nights, in part because of how ridiculous Vancouver traffic gets in the middle of December, but mostly because I'd been trying to get this finale right. Doug was planning to fly in from New York and arrive back home in Burnaby at seven, so I'd asked Siri to remind me to make it home this time. I woke up my phone and read the notification:

REMINDERS: Birthday dinner with Doug tonight, 8 p.m. Don't be late!

Happy birthday to me.

Oh, no.

It's too late. I get it, now. Jill had been trying to keep me away from my office.

Red and yellow streamers hanging from the doorframe attack my reddened face, getting tangled in my long hair. I try to brush them aside, but several rip. Before I can pull them out of my tresses, the TV cast, crew, directors, and producers begin singing "Happy Birthday" to me. Thirty "Happy 30th" balloons, in a rainbow of colors, fill the room, and our executive producer, Stan, is holding a big, round chocolate cake with "Flirty & Thirty, Hannah!" scrawled across the top in pink. Behind him, at the top of a pile of paperwork on my desk, I can see a large, manila envelope addressed to Hannah Storm. Doug's envelope. Doug's divorce papers.

I want to run and hide. This has to be the most awkward moment ever in the history of my existence, except maybe for that one time I raced up on stage to get an Emmy award with the bottom of my glamorous, shimmery black skirt accidentally tucked into the top. Even with all that tucking going on, I still managed to trip up the stairs.

Good Nights

"Happy birrrthdaaay, dear Hannah!" the group encircles me, urging me to blow out the candles. Jill comes up beside me with an odd expression on her face—one that only I can decipher. She pulls half of a red streamer off my shoulder. Then, as everyone else continues singing, she whispers in my left ear, "Your husband wants a divorce, and all we got you was a cake with thirty fucking candles on it."

Thank God for old friends like Jill, for making me chuckle when I believe all I can ever do again is cry. I sigh and close my eyes. I don't know what to wish for.. At thirty, I'm practically ancient by Hollywood's standards, and I have to start all over again. My marriage is over, and there are whispers that my TV show is, too.

I blow out the candles and wish for a miracle.

Two

Hannah

Six months later.

The woman with fake boobs on Fox News looks at the camera like she has information that will shake the very core of my existence. I'm in pink flannel PJs and have a gigantic bowl of Naughty Monkey caramel corn on my lap. If this news is earth shattering, bring it. I'm prepared. I can hunker down like this for days.

"Hannah Storm tweeted today about her devastating divorce from Doug Evan. She wore the most divine fire-engine red Gucci heels to her lunch date in downtown Vancouver, so we can confirm she's over him and onto her next conquest, who may be the director of a new movie she's writing."

"Hannah's heels. Hannah's heels. It's all about Hannah. All about Hannah," our mini-macaw Jughead chortles.

That damn bird. I have cherished him, his green feathers, bright red shoulders, and bold personality for ten years, but in the six months since I've been living alone, he's started to sound exactly like my ex. So, did Doug offer to take Jughead with him to New York, where he moved for good shortly after our split? Of course, he didn't. He took the cat. The cat, which I always adored and considered mine!

I get up from the couch, full of nervous energy after that so-called newscast. Since when did red heels make headlines? I also love how my career made the tail end of the story, while my love life made the top. That glass ceiling won't be shattering any time soon.

I open the red wine on the kitchen counter and pour myself a half glass, then walk over to the window and look outside. Burnaby mountain on the majestic Coastal Mountain range is lit up by its own lights tonight with a round, orange moon and puffy pink clouds above it. It's an awe-inspiring sight, and you'd think it would motivate me to write. I was supposed to be writing tonight. Last night, too. No luck.

When my show, Never Flip a Fried Egg Naked, was canceled and our Vancouver offices closed in April, I thought I could shake the disappointment off and keep writing. Television shows are made and canceled as quickly as people upgrade their cell phones. Ours lasted four years–that's television gold. The network execs told me they felt it was best to say farewell when everyone still loved the characters and the show. It's common practice. So why should I take it personally?

I am taking it personally. Just a smidge. Why? Because the show that is taking the place of mine is geared to a much younger market, with amoeba brains.

My show was about men and women searching for meaning in their thirty-something suburban lives. It was funny and real, with a clever feminist vibe. The show replacing mine, Rate My Wedding, is a contest where couples compete for the most talked-about wedding and a prize of one million dollars. Their wedding days are actually rated by the viewers.

Good Nights

The night before I learned my show was being cancelled, I had flown in to LA to meet with the exec producer, Arnie, and the network CEO, George, for what I thought was going to be a celebration lunch announcing that I'd be writing a fifth season. When George handed me the entire plate of bruschetta and blinked his puny pair of pity-eyes at me, I knew I wasn't going to have an appetite for the rest of the meal. This sucked the life out of me, because I heard the place served a scrumptious blueberry crumble.

"Hannah. Hani." George began.

I wasn't hungry, but still, I stuffed a whole bruschetta in my mouth. I despised when he called me Hani and then prattled on for an hour. This was going to take a while.

"Never Flip A Fried Egg hasn't been renewed. With the main cameraman recently being accused of sexual harassment by cast members…"

Seriously, they were going to go with that? That was their excuse? That had barely made page eighteen news, with so many bigger celebrities in hotter water. It was a serious allegation, and he'd been let go, but puh-lease. This was just Arnie and George, trying to cover up for ageism.

"I heard you're replacing it with a show that features episodes like eighteen-year-old women dancing around in their skimpy underwear at their Stagettes. You're not worried about the kind of tabloid attention that's going to attract?"

"That's a different kind of attention," Arnie said, looking up from his filet mignon for a minute before carefully cutting a small piece of fat off the steak. His knife incised it like a surgeon. Slow, exact. I couldn't help envisioning my heart on that plate. He was cutting me and all I'd ever accomplished out of the picture, because he found it was unnecessary. Tonight, I'd be dog food out in the back alley.

I took a sip of water. "So, this isn't about my show being about feminists. Or that, you know, it has depth."

"Write a movie, Hani. Or maybe even a book," George said, ignoring my question as he often did. "We know you have that in you. Come back to TV when the climate's a little better, sweetheart." With that, he threw his linen napkin on his chair, got up, kissed me on the forehead, and left. Arnie wasn't even paying attention to us. He was still operating on his steak.

The memory of George treating me like a daughter instead of a celebrated industry peer never left me. I simply filed it away for better days—ammunition and inspiration. I may not know much, but if my failed marriage has taught me anything, it's that you have to decide what's important and what's not worth wasting energy on, and through it all, find the funny.

I set out to find my funny-bone again, with little luck. Writing my first screenplay has proved far more difficult than I imagined, and it's not just the mental clutter and self-doubt, or that every Thursday at eight I find myself screaming to my TV set, "Stupid freaking pointless show!" as a gorgeous blonde bride selects her flowers on Rate My Wedding.

My usual writing process simply isn't working in this old space. Jillian was right; I should sell it and get a place of my own. There are too many memories here, and besides, I'm going to need the money if I can't finish and sell this screenplay. At this stage of the game, it's not looking too promising.

Of course, Fox News says I've already got a director on board, for the screenplay I haven't even finished, and I'm probably sleeping with him, so what do I know?

If I'm not careful, my blood pressure is going to go off the charts. I sip my wine and settle back down on the couch. I need to finish this screenplay, but to do that, I need to be funny again. I need to laugh again!

What kind of journalists can't even do proper digging to find out my lunch date was with a real estate agent? He had three apartments for me to look at in LA. I've been trying to decide if LA is the place for me to be, since I'm going to be trying to pitch and sell a movie there. Vancouver may be all everyone's buzzing about on the production side of the industry lately, but LA remains where most of the meetings take place. It doesn't appeal to me as my home base, though. Compared to my life in B.C., it feels congested, plastic, and competitive. I simply met with an agent to consider my options.

When the agent showed me the properties, none of them felt right, so I didn't even bother booking an appointment to look at them. Since it's an international agency, I did ask him to put our Burnaby house up for sale. I need a much bigger change of scenery than moving to Hell-A, and to do that, I need money for airfare and rent.

Maybe I'll end up in downtown Vancouver, eventually, to be close to Mom and Jill, but there's a vast world out there, and new experiences make for better writers. I know it, my BFF has said it, and now I just need to gather the courage to leave this house and never look back.

"Get a grip, Hannah. Get a grip."

I swear Doug trained that freaking bird to say that. He wasn't only mean and abusive, he was vindictive. I don't know why I shoved the knowledge of who he truly is under the carpet for so many years.

It's time to throw caution to the wind. It's time for a new chapter. It's been time since Doug texted me that he wanted a divorce; I just wasn't emotionally ready to leap yet.

I need to head somewhere foreign, and preferably warmer, but first, I'm going to find a loving caretaker for Jughead. Doug is out, of course. I've already begged him to take the bird, and he argues—by text, he never speaks to me in person anymore—that it's my problem.

<The cat followed me home. The bird was a special gift to you. Besides, as I have told you numerous times, my condo here in New York doesn't allow birds.>

I reread the text, wondering why I even bother to keep these hurtful threads on my cell, set down my wine glass, and start punching in Jill's number.

"Boob. Don't be a boob," Jughead shrieks. That's it. Enough is enough.

Jill answers on the first ring. "Hey, I need to get away for a month to write. What are the chances you could take care of Jughead? Like, forever?"

Three

Hannah

I despise that I'm a pathetic softie when it comes to animal welfare. Tough as nails with humans at the bargaining table, but room temperature Jell-O when an animal tips its head to one side and looks at me.

Jill couldn't take Jughead because she's working long hours every day on an LA TV show set. She also can't stand my ex and understandably doesn't want to deal with sarcastic bird comments every day for the next fifteen years. My Mom isn't allowed pets in her apartment. When I thought about whether I could live with myself leaving him at a shelter, the answer came up a resounding no.

"Oh, Mom." I sighed into the phone this morning. "I've made bad life choices."

"Don't be so hard on yourself, honey. We all make mistakes. That's how you grow."

"I guess. I feel like my best friend is a parrot. I never see Jill anymore! Well, there's you, course."

"There are worse things than having a pet as a friend. Pets don't talk back."

"Uh, this one does!"

"He is rather rude. Needs a time out! So then, it's decided? You're taking him? Do you need me to stage the house or is the agent doing that?"

"Oh no, the agent is just showing the place, could you do that for me, Mom? Your flowers and candles magic, with what little furniture is left? Water my plants?" Mom took a home staging course a few years ago, and it turns out she's a flower-arranging, fountain-formation rock star.

"Of course I can. If you wouldn't mind me having a few gals over one night for drinks… it gets quite cramped at my place."

"Sure. Little bit of strip poker?" I tease.

"I think we're far too old for that dear. But you go write in France, and whoop it up, or whatever young people call it these days. You deserve a break."

So, here I am, on my mother's orders, and what was supposed to be a sunny, peaceful, solo writing retreat, standing by the ocean in a cold torrential downpour. Oh, and I'm about to carry a Hahn's mini-macaw onto a ferry leaving France's mainland. Yes, leaving. I certainly hope the weather is nicer on the small island where I'm headed.

At least Jughead is the smallest of his kind, but right now, he sounds like my ex-husband on speed. I should probably see a therapist about my loyalty to this bird, but I don't have time. I have to get this screenplay finished so I can keep my name out there. If I get at least one movie credit to my name, maybe I can get hired back to TV, which is my passion.

Is it? I hate those stuffy awards shows. And the late nights and early mornings writing to deadline. I despise pacing my office floorboards down to sawdust when I can't get an idea for the next episode and it's due that afternoon. I hate being a woman in an industry where women are hardly respected, and even if they are, they're paid less than their male colleagues.

But I love the writing. I love getting lost in the characters and their emotions. I love making people laugh.

Just this morning, I got to experience that feeling again first hand, when I met a viewer in the business lounge.

After rushing around the crowded airport pushing a suitcase and a squawking macaw in my metal cart, getting many strange looks from passersby, I finally had a peaceful moment in the lounge. Jughead was safe in cargo, having been checked by customs, and all his forms were sent to the airport in France. I was assured that, because most European countries don't require quarantine of birds, I would be fine upon our arrival, however, the airport vet had sent notice to the vet at the Charles de Gaulle airport. It was a long flight and took another hour for the vet to check Jughead.

I stare out at the rain-streaked window as the ferry prepares to leave, lost in thought. A whole month alone on a French island. I'll have a house all to myself to relax, to write my movie, and to retrain this bird to sound like me again. Sure. It's possible. I googled it, so I know it must be true.

I feel optimistic and grateful that the house owner let me bring my macaw. This bird is beautiful and rare, and it was a group gift from my first television crew. He poops a lot and makes a screeching noise worse than a colicky baby when he's angry, but he represents how far I've come in my career. I can't just dump Jughead at some shelter, even if he has become a cheeky teenager.

I wanted to stay at a fancy five-star hotel in Cannes, but none of them would accept the parrot. I kept saying that it was the size of a cockatiel and well-behaved—I lied about that part—but they wouldn't budge.

Thankfully, Jill introduced me to the Good Nights app, and that's how I found a lovely home for rent for a month on the little-known Ile Saint Bruno, south of Cannes, off the coast of France. The house owner, James, said it would be fine to keep Jughead in his cage in the living room. I'll have my privacy on a gorgeous, under-populated island. I know I can finish my screenplay here. I'll be done in a few weeks, and, thanks to my connections in TV, I can have it sold a month later. I'll be back on my feet again before the end of summer.

And now, thanks to a serendipitous meeting in the airport, I feel encouraged to write again.

"Oh my, that is the funniest show I've seen in a long time," the woman at the table beside me was dabbing the corners of her eyes and chuckling. "I've been binge watching this for hours." She turned to me and showed me her tablet. She was watching my show, Never Flip A Fried Egg Naked on Netflix, and didn't even realize I was the creator. That happened a lot lately. I smiled at her.

"What's your favorite part so far?" I asked, taking another sip of my Chardonnay.

"Oh, well, it'll make you blush," she smirked, her cheeks round and rosy. I could tell she'd enjoyed several glasses of wine.

"I doubt it, since I wrote it." I smiled at her, then sat back and soaked in the surprised and joyful expression on her face.

"Oh, my! I thought you looked a little like Hannah Storm. This is something! Oh. Well, now I need your autograph." She handed me a pad and pen. "To Marjorie."

"Only if you tell me what made you blush, Marjorie."

"Ha! Well. I loved that Carly couldn't… you know… she was feeling unsexy. And old. I could relate! So, her husband Drake takes her out for dinner and lots of wine, and then, just before stores start closing…"

"They do it in an office supply store," I said, breaking into a grin.

"On the fancy desks and leather chairs! And a young shelf stocker boy finds them and can't break them apart!" Marjorie was laughing so hard, tears were streaming from her eyes.

I sighed. It was the validation I needed. I knew then that I had to keep writing. I had my audience after all. Maybe I'd had them all along. I just needed a change of scenery.

"Rock the boat, baby. Rock the boat," Jughead squawks.

I'm trying to get comfortable on the wooden bench inside this small, eight-car ferry with Jughead in his cage beside me. We're experiencing what I'd call major turbulence, with dark grey skies and high winds, but I'm doing my best to convince myself it's just an ordinary crossing between Cannes and the Island.

Jughead's comment was spot on for the moment. Did I play that song for him recently? I can't recall. I'm always fascinated by what he retains and what I can never get him to say, no matter how many times I say it. It will be interesting to discover what I can and can't teach him once I spend more time alone with him.

"*Pardonnez-moi, madame, voulez-vous d'aide avec votre valise*?" A tanned, broad-shouldered gentleman wearing the ferryboat logo on his t-shirt hands me a card, takes my suitcase in his right hand and the cage in his left, and smiles at me. The card reads, "Ferry Taxi. 24 heures." Smart. He works on and off the ferry. Still, there are a dozen people getting off this ferry, and he approached me. Perhaps the ferry workers saw my nervous expression when the waves started getting wild, and they want to make it up to me. Maybe the house owner arranged this. If everyone is this helpful on Ile St. Bruno, I'm going to enjoy my stay immensely.

"*Oui, merci*," is about all the French I know, but I nod, hand him a slip of paper with the address where I'm headed, and follow him off the boat. The house owner said it was only a two-minute walk to his place from where the ferries come in, however, it would be up a hill. I notice my helper far ahead of me, loading an electric car, so I walk down the platform to the boardwalk and take in the idyllic scene.

I'm nervous to be in this new place, but mostly, I'm feeling excited to be trying something new. Soaking wet and feeling chilled, but excited.

The sky is overcast, but it's finally stopped raining. Swaying palm trees line the boardwalk, and beyond the winding highway that stretches along the ocean, lush rolling hills are dotted with cream colored, red-roofed homes. I've read that Ile St. Bruno isn't popular with many tourists, yet. It's divided into sprawling mansions like these that only celebrities can afford to rent, an old coniferous forest at its center, and on the other side of the island, there's a downtrodden, poverty-stricken area of homes built mostly as cottages in the 1930s and 1940s. The French government supported the upkeep of that stretch of a hundred or so homes until the turn of the century, when they decided it was more lucrative for them to pump money into high-tourist towns along the French Riviera.

Once ushered inside the car, I catch my breath and try to dry off my wet face with my scarf. I'll have to check a mirror once inside; I'm sure I look like a wet cocker spaniel.

As I peer out the window, I notice that every home on the hillside before me has a balcony looking over the ocean and an arched set of double glass doors leading inside. This is more beautiful than any Malibu beach town. It's already quieter than both Vancouver and LA. I can hear the seagulls cry and the ocean roar, unlike in stateside ocean towns, where noisy traffic takes over.

As we pull off the road, I soak in the stunning architecture of the house at the end of this long, paved driveway. It shares elements of French mansions I've seen on earlier vacations, but also reminds me of a Moroccan ease, from the lazy river weaving along its side to its yellow stucco walls, its curvy cast-iron balconies, its sky-blue shutters, and French doors covered in loose white sheers blowing freely in the breeze. I want to stay here more than a month. It already feels like home.

There's no turning back, now. It's fine. This is one of the most adventurous ideas I've had in a while. I've never stayed in someone else's home before, and I've never been alone in a foreign country.

I know that lately I've been lacking a sense of adventure in my life. I certainly wasn't to blame for Doug leaving me. I heard through the industry grapevine that he met a younger brunette two years ago who played a significant role in that story. Still, I realize that I also fell into a pattern of working long hours, and then feeling too tired to do anything fun with him on the weekends. I said 'no' far too many times to events I later realized I would have enjoyed if I'd even given them a second thought. I was afraid of going out of my comfort zone.

Now, I'm way out of that zone, about to start a new adventure on a French island. I am A Superwoman of Change. I'm soaked, my toes feel like icicles, my new bra is cutting into my ribs, and my thong's giving me a wedgie, but Superwoman, honey, that's my hashtag.

I bend down and search under the woven grass doormat for the key. Huh? James said he'd leave the key right here. Where is it?

Did I get the day wrong? What's going on? Should I knock on the door? That's ludicrous, right? No one will answer, don't be silly. But, I think I hear noises inside. Oh, right. The cleaner. James said if there was no key, the cleaner would likely be inside, and she'd let me in.

I give the glass door a rap with my knuckles and wave my driver to walk farther up to the steps, so he can set down my luggage and Jughead behind me. I don't want him holding all that weight the whole time we're waiting.

Five more minutes pass. Damnit, I'm frozen, and I have to pee.

"Hello?"

I wait a minute.

"Can someone answer the door!" I say, a little too loudly.

There. I hear movement! Someone's coming to the door. Everything is going to be fine. More than fine. I just know it.

"Answer the fucking door," Jughead squawks.

Oh, Jughead!

Four

Tripp

The woman in the black dress, cardigan and red heels standing at the front door looks like a beautiful French model turned-crazy-fortune-teller. Her head is wrapped in a long, sheer black scarf, and there's a burly man behind her, holding what looks to be a small parrot in a cage. Her jet-black mascara is dripping from the corners of her bright green eyes, all the way down her cheeks in four wavy lines. Her dark ginger hair is matted, dripping wet and flat against her head.

"Hello?" I brace myself for a string of strange French words, but they don't come.

"Hi. You're the owner? I didn't think you actually lived here. I thought I had the place to myself?" She gets out her phone and opens an app.

"I beg your pardon?"

"I'm renting here for a month? We messaged on Good Nights."

She shoves the phone under my nose, but the rain is coming down so hard, it's spotting and fogging up the screen. I certainly don't want company, but the look on this woman's face tells me she could completely snap if I turn her away. I wouldn't want to be an accomplice.

"I'm sorry, I've already rented this place for the month. You've probably got the wrong address, but if you want to come in from the rain…."

Before I can help her inside, she grabs the door with one hand and marches into the front foyer, pulling a red suitcase behind her. The burly man follows her, puts down the cage, gives her a little nod, and she hands him forty Euros. He hurries back down the stairs and long driveway to his car, seemingly eager to leave this situation. As am I, except, it seems that I'm stuck with a strange woman and her bird in the foyer of a house where I'd been promised solitude.

As the stunning red-shouldered bird begins squawking—rather angrily, for a macaw, I must say—the woman pulls a canary yellow cage cover out of her suitcase and begins to drape it over him.

"Sorry, he's really stressed out right now. This will calm him." She bends down to talk to him in a soothing voice before completely covering the cage. Her hair is dripping all over the wood floor.

"So, your Hahn's macaw is stressed out…but you're just peachy?" I cross my arms over my chest and smirk, resisting the sudden urge to wipe the mascara off her face for her. If she's indeed American, as I suspect from her accent, my kind gesture might be interpreted as creepy. Besides, I like her haggard, far from perfect look. The women at the museum where I work in Oxford wear up-dos and so much makeup they look like they're about to attend the opera at eight a.m.

"I've had better days." She sighs and smiles up at me. "Better months, actually."

She has the face of an angel when she smiles like that. "Sorry to hear that. Well, come on in, uh…"

"Hannah. Hannah Storm, from Vancouver. You know your birds."

"Hello, Hannah. Yes, I'm an ornithologist. Always wanted to go to Vancouver. Never have been. I suppose they have no need for an ornithologist in a city like that do they… 'though I hear there are a variety of beautiful birds in Stanley Park." Bugger, I'm going on now, and sounding like a muppet. I don't want her staying here. Just get her dry and on her way.

"Sorry. I'm Tripp. Tripp Wilson, from Oxford. Here, let me take your scarf, and that cardigan is soaked." I take everything from her hands and grab her suitcase. I don't want her to stay, but I can't have her catching a cold, either.

"Will your birdy be fine here for now?" I cannot believe that sentence just came out of my mouth. There are far too many street meanings for that word, none of them proper. Why, why did I let that slip from my lips? I feel my cheeks grow hot and glance over at her. She's snickering.

"My birdy, Jughead, probably wants some company." She takes off her heels, lifts the cage without even grunting, and follows me.

I motion for her to set the cage down beside the couch in the living room, where there's already a fire on. It's an unusually chilly afternoon for late May. I'm hoping it warms up, so I can go bird-watching without needing a hat and gloves early tomorrow.

"It's okay, girl," I sit down in the recliner and give Coffee a scratch under her ears. She's slowly coming out of her deep sleep at my feet. She's so deaf, none of the commotion in the foyer disturbed her. "This is my lab, Coffee."

Hannah is sitting in a stiff position on the couch, phone on her knees, staring without blinking at Coffee and me.

"So. It seems that you brought your macaw, and I brought my Chocolate lab," I say. "They need to change the name of that app to Bad Nightmares."

"That's not funny." She scowls at me. "How can you have booked with Good Nights? They only take one lodger here at a time. Are you certain you booked with them?"

"Well, I did, and yet, it appears we're both here. With pets."

"Don't state the obvious!" She looks flustered as she scrolls through her phone, searching for something.

"I'm sorry…" I don't know why I just said that. She's the one who has obviously made a mistake. Instead of raising her voice, she should be apologizing to me, for storming into my rental home like she has.

"This is unbelievable. It's like when American Airlines' computers had a glitch, and no pilots were scheduled to fly planes over the Christmas holidays. The computers assigned them all vacations for the same week, so there was no one scheduled to fly!" She stands up and starts pacing the floor.

"I don't see how this is like that," I say. "That company found that glitch. They fixed it. Clearly, Good Nights isn't aware of this glitch."

"Well then." She hands me her phone. Her Good Nights app is open, with the dates she should be staying here highlighted. They are my exact dates, barring the two days I've been here alone.

"Bugger me sideways. We're booked here on the same dates."

"Bugger you, how?" She laughs.

I shrug, ignoring her question. She can look it up in her Guidebook to Brits, which I'm quite sure she didn't bother to purchase.

"You've been here a day already?" she asks.

"No, two…" I study the calendar again. "I suppose they booked me in first."

"Then you need to contact them. Or the owner. Or both of them, I don't know…" She begins pacing again.

"Ah, and why am I the one who has to contact them? You seem fully self-sufficient, having booked your trip on this app, then traveled all the way here from Vancouver. My secretary booked my stay here…"

Hannah stops pacing, sighs, and puts her hands at her hips.

"Of course, she did. I know… your… your… your type."

"You do, do you?" I dislike her tone, but let's see where she's going.

"You're a famous British scientist—you already told me you study birds. You're staying here on a big grant, obviously. You're used to the institution you work for—a university maybe?—doing everything for you. And your wife. She does everything for you, too. Just look… your sweater's on backwards."

I glance down at my dark grey jumper, see she's correct, but don't adjust it. I was in a rush to get studying this morning, is all. "That's presumptuous…" I'm incensed she'd make such assumptions within our first five minutes together. "I do work at the Oxford University museum. And yes, the staff is a great help to me. Someone at the museum did help arrange my stay here so I could search for an elusive bird, once thought extinct. But, no, I'm not some mad scientist who can't find matching socks or brew his own tea." I swallow hard. I'm not going to reply to the wife comment. She doesn't deserve a reply.

"In fact, would you like a cup right now? Anything to get those knickers out of that knot."

"Woah. My knickers are not in a..." she frowns, folds her arms across her chest, turns to the fire, and then bends to partially uncover the bird cage. The macaw peeks out and gives us a surreptitious glance, then hides again. Cheeky fellow. I like the bird. I'm not so sure about her.

"I'm fine. I'm just upset that we're both here, when this was supposed to be a solo holiday for me, away from everything."

"You're an actress, aren't you?" I ask quickly. "I don't watch many American or Canadian films or shows... but you look the part. And I hear this island is a popular spot for celebrities."

She turns to look at me and purses her lips. I can't tell if she's flattered or angry, until she speaks. "Oh, so now it's your turn to make assumptions. The dress, heels, scarf... that was just to feel... sexy again." She's blushing slightly. "I've been writing for months in sweatpants and old t-shirts. I just wanted to make an effort in public. I'm not an actress. I write words for them, though."

"A screenwriter?" Bugger me. So, she lives the celebrity lifestyle. Probably spoiled rotten. Fed with the silver spoon. Can't have her staying here.

"Television, mostly. I had a show that did well in the U.S. for a while, but it was recently canceled. I'm here to finish a screenplay... er... start it, actually. It hasn't been going very well."

"Sorry to hear that." I don't see the point of making small talk anymore. One of us has to offer to leave. I need to prove that the Skinks Babbler isn't extinct, and I only have a small window to do so. How can I convince her she doesn't want to stay?

"Alright, why don't you sit down again, and let's try to contact these people at Good Nights. See if we can get you a refund."

Coffee suddenly gets up and stares at me. She starts whimpering.

"Bad dog! Bad dog!" Jughead squeals.

Hannah sighs and moves Jughead's cage so he can't see the dog. I let Coffee jump up beside me and give her a comforting rub.

"I don't need a refund if I can just stay here as planned." She says it slowly, calculating, and remains standing.

"I was here first." I glare at her, and she glares back. Ah yes, there it is. She may look like an angel, but she's cunning, hard-headed, selfish, and she wants my rental.

Why did I offer her goddamn tea?

Five

Hannah

I haven't liked much that's come out of Tripp Wilson's mouth this entire time, except when he offered me tea. I could really use a cup. He offered. Was he serious? Or, is he playing a game here, too?

I sit down again, hoping that the strength of my stare might weaken him. It was once a great advantage point for me in negotiating my TV pay.

I can't decide who is more put out by our unusual situation. The top of his ears are bright red, and his cheeks are pink. He's exhaling deeply, stroking his sandy brown stubble beard and mustache, running his hands through his wavy hair. I'd say he's a little stressed, and I'm the cause.

Even in this flustered state, and with that silly sweater on backwards, he's ruggedly handsome, there's no denying that. He has an adventurous, rebellious sparkle in those electric blue eyes, which is unexpected, considering he's a scientist. I had the impression that scientists were dull; then again, a lot of people say that about writers. Careers don't make the person.

Alright, he's good-looking and clever, so what? I'm here to get work done. Besides, he's been nothing but egocentric and rude to me, except for when he took my wet "cardigan," as he called it, and offered the tea. He did do those things for me. In fact, he's just broken our staring contest, and now he's standing up...

"Right, then. We're two professionals, both on this island for equally important work. I suppose we should be more civilized about this. I'm going to the kitchen, and let's try again when we've had our tea and fairy cakes, shall we?"

I look down at my lap and try to hide my giggles. Tea and fairy cakes certainly sounds like a step in the right direction. Magical, even. Still! He's in my rental home, and he wants me to give up my right to stay here. British academic snob.

Once I hear Tripp rustling about in the kitchen, I use the time to scroll through Good Nights to see if there are any notifications about app errors. I can't scroll past the calendar we were just looking at. It seems to be frozen on the calendar and a sidebar I saw twelve hours ago, when I last logged in to check the address, but the time and notifications are all still the same. Strange.

When I close the app, it remains frozen, and I have to delete it entirely from my phone and re-upload it before doing anything else. Even with the new upload, the date and time are still frozen! This is a nightmare. I'm going to have to search their number, call, and find out what's going on. I'll have to keep using data on my phone. Damn. I already paid a ridiculous amount for this international package. I could really use the Wi-Fi password right now, which I can't get because I don't have access to my Good Nights messages. Still, I'm trying to get on his good side... I'll wait.

First, I google the island-to-Cannes ferry service. Maybe if I book his ticket, make it easy for him, he'll let me have the place. Cannes has lovely hotels, he can just book a room there. He's a Brit, aren't they always chivalrous?

The next ferry doesn't leave until tomorrow, at eight a.m., thankfully, there are two bedrooms and two bathrooms here. Lots of space for the both of us. I just hope there's space for his ego, too.

Tripp returns with his sweater on properly, a tray of teacups, a teapot, white frosted cupcakes, and small, round sponge cakes. He calls them crumpets. I've heard about these but haven't ever tried them.

"Cream? Sugar?" I nod, so he pours me a cup of tea, adds the cream and sugar, gives it a stir with a small spoon, then hands it to me with a crumpet on the saucer.

"Thank you. This looks delicious." I smile, then add, "Bad news. The app froze on me, and I had to delete it to get my phone working again.

"The app is buggered. It gets a bad rap from me," he says.

"Bad app. Bad rap. Bad bad rap," Jughead cackles under his cover.

Tripp chuckles, shaking his head. "He's certainly entertaining..." He glances at Coffee to check on her. She's fast asleep beside the recliner.

"He is that. I suppose it's ridiculous to some people that I'd take my macaw on vacation..."

"Hey, I love birds, they're my life's work. However, it does seem a rather far journey for you both..."

"Well…" I sip the Earl Grey. He added just the right amount of cream and sugar. It takes like dessert in a cup. "I'm recently divorced. I needed to get far away."

"Oh?" He sits down slowly in the recliner, holding my gaze.

"Yes. It was building for years, I suppose, but the way it came... it was a shock. So, I know what being abandoned feels like, and I wouldn't want to do that to an innocent creature. Even if he is a noisy, cheeky bird, he's mine, and I wanted to take care of him." I look down at my lap. "I've sort of been married to my work these last few years. Haven't had much time for a social life. But, my show was recently canceled, so, as it turns out, this feathered noisemaker is one of the few friends I've got."

Holy overshare, Hannah. Why did you just spill your life story to a stranger?

Six

tripp

I glance at the antique gold wristwatch Maggie gave me and try not to roll my eyes as Hannah finishes her long and drawn out story about why she's sitting opposite me today.

Of course, she doesn't have many friends. She's a spoiled North American princess, flying to France on a whim, living the high life of a celebrity. I bet she's never done a hard day's labor in her life. She seems nice enough, but self-absorbed. She hasn't even asked me what my work entails.

Perhaps I'm being a little harsh. Divorce is always sad, and I definitely feel for her sense of loss. But, she thinks she knows my type? How dare she assume I'm like every British academic on the planet? I bet she hasn't even met another one. She's probably basing her impression of me on some Hugh Laurie film or worse, every James Bond character ever created.

Hannah turns quiet. She seems to be enjoying the crumpets. I get up, stretch, and throw another log on the fire, taking time to inhale the smoky ash as the sparks fly. When I turn, I catch her looking at my face. I don't look away, but I don't crack a smile. She can't win. I need this space to myself for a month, so I can find that bird and prove everyone wrong. I definitely won't locate it with Princess Hannah yabbering at me all day long.

When she finally breaks the silence, I notice she has finished an entire cup of tea and is pouring herself another. "So, who was this Saint Bruno this island was named after, anyway? I've never heard of him. 'Course I'm a lapsed Catholic..."

"Well, you're lucky. I had to go to Bible school back in Kent for three whole summers. I can explain." I push the log on the grill one more time, get up from my crouched position, and hang the poker with the other steel fireplace tools. We're silent for a moment, admiring the crackling fire. I daren't bring up the app just yet. Maybe if I can get her to warm to me, I can convince her that since I was here first, she should sod off and leave me in peace. I sit back down in my recliner and catch her glancing my way again. She quickly looks away, down to her phone.

"You know, I could just Google it..."

"You do seem rather attached to that phone of yours," I say. "Do you ever just turn it off?"

She frowns at me. "I'm not addicted, if that's what you're asking."

"I didn't mean to imply..." I say. Bugger. She doesn't appear to be warming up to me.

"I just wonder if people even remember what they did before apps." I try again, though I'm not sure why. "Say, Good Nights. What did people do before Good Nights got popular?"

"I think people stayed in motels, with questionable stains on the comforters."

I bite my lower lip to avoid laughing. Damn, she's brazen. Clever and funny. This isn't going to be as easy as I thought. I don't want her to have the upper hand.

"I spend a lot of time in the field, birdwatching, even camping out there some nights. I suppose I've grown accustomed to logging off from society for a few days. It brings me a sense of peace."

"Yea, well, I just wanted to be alone, writing a screenplay, in this home. That would have been peaceful." She sighs, and I realize my hospitality hasn't done one thing to change her mind. She wants to stay, and she wants me gone. Bugger me. Maybe I can impress her with my knowledge of St. Bruno.

"Right, then. Here's what I know—Bruno and his friends built an oratory in France, with small individual cells. They met for prayers every day and spent the rest of their time in solitude, eating together only for great feasts. Their main work was copying manuscripts. As a result, a lot of French writers come to this island. In fact, I thought you were one at first, until you started speaking with an American accent."

"West-coast Canadian, to be exact, and holy stream of factoids, Factman. I could really use you when I'm researching my screenplay. Are you some kind of genius?"

I chuckle and take a sip of tea before answering. "I'm more the Jack of all Trades type. I know random facts that likely don't matter in the end, but I've been like that since I was a kid. I also know far too much about one elusive bird—the Short-tailed Skinks Babbler."

"The Short-tailed Skinks Babbler?" She giggles. "I'd be hiding too, with a name like that."

She laughs, but at least she's finally talking about my work. This is a pleasant surprise. I suppose my first impression was somewhat unforgiving. Perhaps she simply had too much on her mind before.

"So, you're confident you can find it here?" she asks.

"It's more of a hunch. I mean, I've done the research, and the reports and sightings are convincing, but there's no photographic proof that this bird is still living. It's been reportedly seen in what some call "the last European rainforest," in the Canary Islands off Morocco, and in the coniferous forest here, and that's it. I want to try here first. Others have already searched for it in the Canary Islands and failed."

"So, your career is resting on this one finding?"

"Kind of. Mostly. Yes," I answer.

"Oh. Well, I can relate. I won't have any income coming in after August. Except if my show stays on Netflix, but that won't be enough to pay rent when I get a new place. I signed a prenup, so I'm pretty much back to where I started when I got married. Our home is up for sale, but it hasn't sold yet. Most of our furniture and my entire bedroom set has gone to storage. My divorce was both an emotional and financial setback."

"So, you're trying to tell me that you're homeless and your career is resting on writing a winning screenplay here?"

"Kind of. Mostly. Yes."

Bloody hell. I was hoping she'd say she could write it elsewhere. Can't she? "But the bird is somewhere on this island. I need to be here. Can't you write anywhere in the world?" I catch her eyes. She blinks at me, looks down at her lap, and then looks up again.

"I really don't want to, but you do make a good argument for yourself, and you were here first. I can leave first thing in the morning."

That was quick. I thought she'd put up more of a fight. Or, is this some kind of female trickery? I remember Maggie doing this sometimes. She'd do something my way, but look so bloody glum about it I'd feel obliged to back down.

I can see her swallowing hard, and her eyes are filling with tears. Oh no. She was just divorced, she lost her show and her financial stability, she isn't sure where she's going to live… and now I've gone and made her cry.

Damn it woman! Don't cry. I am not falling for this. No bloody way! I have a sob story too, we all do. You don't see me crying because I might lose my vacation rental.

"That's great, Hannah, thank you kindly, but do stay on. Stay a couple days—at least, until you've found somewhere nice on the mainland."

She sighs a sweet little sound of relief that's strange music to my ears, then smiles up at me.

What have I just said? What did I just do? Have I gone mad? I just heard myself invite her to stay on.

Blasted reflex! Mum always taught me to be a kind host, to respect women at all times, but this is bloody ridiculous. I absolutely need to work alone on my research findings, yet I've just invited a spoiled Canadian princess to share my precious living space.

I take the tray from the coffee table and turn to walk to the kitchen. "Hopefully we will hear from the app developers soon, and they'll give you that refund which you can use to cover your new rental." I call over to her from the kitchen to the living room. Say it, Tripp. Say it now or regret it always. "So, that way, you can leave even earlier. And I'll help you sort it all out."

She doesn't respond. I wish I could see her expression. I look around the door to see how she's reacting to my proposition.

"Why don't we turn on the telly and see what's going on? Maybe it's happening to more people? Possible?"

She sighs and picks up the remote off the coffee table, and I go back to my work at the sink. "I couldn't even get a message through to Good Nights because the app froze on me," she calls to me. "Usually I stream all my news online, but since my phone's data is so very low, I guess I'll have to put on the news."

I hear her sigh heavily, and the television comes on. That was one incredibly non-subtle hint for the Wi-Fi password. No bloody way she gets the Wi-Fi password. Wi-Fi password equals long term guest.

She who gets the Wi-Fi password wins the war!

I hear a muffled female voice announcing the news from the other room and start loading up the dishwasher. I can't help but think to myself, "Ding, round one, Wilson!" I'm fully expecting another round soon, of course. She'll fire back with some sob story, pull out all the punches, and guilt me into leaving.

If I stay strong, this little boxing match of wits ends first thing tomorrow morning.

Seven

Hannah

This is the BBC. It's not fake news. So, what I'm hearing is true? Is this actually true?

"Hey, come quick. It's about Good Nights!" I still can't believe what I'm hearing.

Tripp is fast to join me on the couch. He's wiping his hands on a lilac dish towel, and as I quickly glance at him, then back to the TV, I'm warmed and surprised by how domestic he looks. It's an odd feeling, because once again I'm realizing my impression of scientists was completely based on stereotypes. He seems to have been enjoying himself, serving me crumpets and cleaning up after our tea.

"The CEO of Good Nights says they're still looking into the problem." The female anchor on BBC continues, "From what they can tell so far, this is a world-wide glitch, and it's wreaking a lot of havoc with its users booked into apartments and homes around the world."

"Bugger me sideways with a chainsaw! It's the roommate apocalypse!" Tripp laughs and looks my way, his brows raised.

"You have the strangest expressions. So, which one of us is the giant meteorite?" I attempt a smile.

"Good Nights is, I guess. And as to my cursing, I simply choose to be more creative than dropping the F-bomb."

"Well, so far, you get a ten in Creative Expression from me. I have to admit, I'm an uncreative curser. I'm surrounded by people in the industry who use the F-bomb every fourth word. I'll have to take lessons from you."

He thinks for a second, then smiles. "Well, I started using bird names to curb my cursing. I read this fantastic book by a renowned psychologist. It worked."

"Really?"

"Sure. Wank, bugger, blasted—they're quite acceptable here, and when you add in a bird name, it slips off your tongue in such a satisfying way. You'll be surprised. Go ahead. Try it. Curse…" He searches for an idea. "The President of the United States. Do it."

I grin. I can only think of one bird at the moment. "He's a wankpuffin."

"There you go! You're a natural." He chuckles and looks about to give me a high-five but walks away to check the fire instead. "So, any luck reaching Good Nights?" he asks over his shoulder.

"Nope, and now their lines will be flooded with calls for at least twenty-four hours. Although, I'm sure we'll be getting refunds, regardless as to who stays where. Or we'll be part of a large class action suit, eventually."

"I'm not getting involved in one of those. They can keep my money." Tripp stands up and walks to the fire, and I notice that his shoulders have stiffened.

The anchor has turned to a young weatherman. "So, besides unusually cool and rainy days, we're watching out for high winds…" Tripp grabs the remote and turns off the TV. He looks irritated.

"What is it? The shi… er, goosey weather, or you don't believe in class actions?"

He slowly turns from the glowing fire to look at me. His playful expression has darkened. "I've had some painful experience with law suits. I wouldn't want to do it again, no." He wrings the dish towel that's in his hands, then tosses it over one shoulder. I want to press him to tell me more, but he turns away again and lifts up my suitcase from beside the couch.

"How about I show you where you can sleep? You must be exhausted after your long flight and then the trek out here to the island. I can make us some supper for say, six?"

I nod, completely taken aback. He just said "us" as though he's going to try to make a go of this odd arrangement, at least for a few days.

"That gives you time to call your… kids? Tell them about the situation. There's an en-suite bathroom if you want to freshen up."

"Oh—no kids," I say point blank because I'm eager to see how he reacts. I'm used to people expecting me to have had them by now, but I've stopped adding any kind of excuse after saying I'm childless. Maybe I'll get to it, maybe I won't. It doesn't make me selfish or any less of a woman, despite that I hear that all the time.

"Right. Seems your cheeky parrot is more than enough for the time being. I feel that way about Coffee sometimes. She'd be awfully jealous of me becoming a dad."

He's a devoted dog owner, doesn't judge me based on my womb status, and he cooks? Hard to believe how many talents this man has.

So, no kids, but he didn't answer me when I asked about a wife. He doesn't wear a ring. He's smart, sexy, skilled. It's surprising no one has scooped him up. Hmm… I'm starting to see the benefits of both of us staying here.

Stop thinking that! I don't want company. I need to spend the next month here, writing alone.

"Dinner would be lovely," I hear a strange part of myself reply; the part that believes men are generally good, and that I could use one in my life.

Wait a sec, Han. You're being swayed by his grace and charm. You're forgetting that there's a game going on here. It's obvious, he's in need of a vacation, and I'm supposed to feel sorry for him, charmed by his accent and those electric blue eyes, so that I let him have the place to himself. He's good. He's really good.

But I'm not going to fall for it. He already insinuated that I'm a spoon-fed celebrity type. Ha! If he only knew how difficult it's been working as a woman trying to get a break in this industry.

I've got this. I'll impress him with my sparkling personality, blow him away with my…okay, truthfully, I haven't impressed many people with my personality lately. There has been zero sparkle. Jillian actually told me that I darkened a room like Death and its scythe whenever I walked in.

But, that's about to change. I saw how Tripp looks at me. He may like his privacy, but I'm pretty sure he's attracted to me. I can convince him to let me stay on. I know I can.

Eight

Hannah

As I stand, stretch my arms over my head, and truly take in my surroundings for the first time since I arrived, I know for certain I want to stay here to write my movie. It's a large, airy space and decorated in light whites and blues in a relaxed, French-country style. There are antique replicas, or actual Victorian pieces, at every turn, but the place doesn't feel stuffy, dark, or ornate. It's eclectic and welcoming. I'm right at home.

There's also plenty of room for the both of us here. I can get my work done on the second level, and Tripp can work, well… wherever he works. That doesn't matter. I've known him, what, two hours? What matters is my work. I'm the one without an income here. He seems to be doing just fine. I bet he'll be feasting on tea and crumpets for decades thanks to his research grant.

Tripp motions me to walk gently past a sleeping Coffee and Jughead's covered cage, so I grab my heels and he leads the way, carrying my suitcase up the dark hardwood stairs, down a long hallway, to one of the two rooms I must have seen from the driveway.

"We'll have to leave Jughead in the living room, at the owner's request," he says, turning on the bedroom light, and I realize it's already grown dark outside. "I'll uncover him for you soon, though. Let's just get him habituated to the sounds and smells of his new environment first."

Spoken like a true Birdman. I smile at his new secret nickname. Jillian calls me Sorting Hannah, as if I'm always wearing Harry Potter's Sorting Hat, because I analyze things and give them strange nicknames. I'll probably be naming the house next; I just need a bit more time.

I can tell that it won't take me long to get used to anything here. This room is perfect for me. It's a large, bright bedroom with a massive, dark oak, four poster carved Queen Tudor bed covered in a cream white quilt. The blue and cream wallpaper is adorned with Victorian drawings of blue and pink ribbons and birds—I think they're swallows. I notice the frosted-glass French doors leading to the balcony right away and can imagine relaxing with my coffee out here, if this rain ever stops.

"I cannot believe what we are paying for this place," I say, realizing my mistake right away. Now he'll know I want to stay longer.

He sets my suitcase down beside a full-length oak mirror that matches the bed, and I toss my heels beside it. I cannot wait to take off this achingly uncomfortable bra and slip into a hot bath.

"It's a steal, that's for sure," he says. "Too bad about all of this, this… Bad Nightmare." He gestures to the phone in my hand. "Maybe you can return mid-summer, once I'm gone."

So, that's that. He really thinks I'm going to give this up so easily? Oh, he doesn't know Hannah Storm.

"Here's your en-suite, for the evening," he continues, emphasizing evening, and opens a frosted glass door to a bright white bathroom with a large, deep, round soaker tub in the corner. "James, the owner, says he renovated all the bathrooms last year. Also, there's a lovely French woman, Béatrice, who comes in twice a week, cleans, adds fresh towels. I haven't met James yet. I suppose I should notify him about this mix-up, but Good Nights should really be the one contacting him."

"I can send him an email, no prob, but I'd like the Wi-Fi password, please."

"Sure, sure, I'll get to that." He walks past me briskly, straight out of the room, then turns, leaning against the doorframe for a moment. "Look, you know where the kitchen is, so you can go make yourself something to eat whenever."

Wait, what?

What just happened? He doesn't want to prepare dinner for me now. He changed his mind in the space of two minutes?

Ah. Right. He's trying to make my stay unpleasant, so I leave sooner. He saw how much I love the room and realized he was in trouble. He needed to up the ante...

What a brat! A clever, delicious tea-making brat, but still a brat. Well, two can play at this game...

I sit on the bed, then bring up my legs and lie back against the pillows, making myself uber-comfortable in front of him, and flashing a little bit of thigh. I'm fluffing up a pillow in its cream, eyelet-patterned sham when I hear a familiar ring coming from his pocket—it's a vid-call. I didn't even realize that he had his own cellphone, let alone that he was the Facetiming type. What is it about this guy? Bit of a mystery, here. He certainly keeps his cards close to his chest.

He's staring at me, not even moving, biting his lower lip, before running his hands through his thick brown waves. Calculating. I'm doing the same, although I don't think it's as obvious as his blue eyes looking intently at mine.

His call gives me time to decide what the... owl... my next move is, since I have absolutely no gagging gull of an idea. I'm trying to get a man I'm not sure I even like to like me, and I'm using bird names in my cursing, essentially for his benefit.

What is going on with me? How long can jet lag affect a person?

"Aren't you going to answer that?" I ask, calmly, smiling up at him as if I'm not the least bit disappointed that he has rescinded his dinner invitation.

"Yup." He finally looks away, pulls the phone from his pocket to answer it, and walks out into the hallway. "Hey, don't make yourself at home," he calls back up to me as he makes his way downstairs. "I mean, I'm sure Good Nights will contact you tonight, with a reservation for you elsewhere."

Don't make yourself at home? I hug the pillow, chuckling softly into it. I do believe I just won that round. Now he's grasping at straws. And such a grumpy crumpet!

Nine

Tripp

I answer the Facetime call and quickly take it downstairs.

I can't see anyone yet, but I'm hearing audio. "Wilson here," I say.

Coffee greets me at the foot of the stairs, wagging her tail, and I give her a swift scratch under the chin.

"Tripp. You don't have to say your name, I can see your mangy face, mate."

I chuckle and take a seat at the edge of the recliner as Evan Canning appears on screen. He's my lab assistant and field technician of the last six years, and the friend who helped me get back to work and the real world when I just about gave up on living.

"I'm glad you answered. I'm not going to be able to make it out there." He frowns.

Evan is never late, and usually, he's quite predictable. I've seen his closet. He's the guy at the museum who only owns white dress shirts and dark pants, so he doesn't waste any time deciding what he's going to wear under his lab coat.

"Oh, no. What's happened?"

"Haven't you heard? There's a storm watch for the entire coast of France. I was sure you… oh right. You never check your bloody weather app. Or your blasted messages, for that matter." He shakes his head.

"Right." I chuckle at the dig, because he's absolutely right. "Can you make it tomorrow, then?" I desperately need his help when I'm out searching the forest tomorrow. It's not a one-man job. My heart swells as I think of Maggie: big brown eyes, floppy red rain hat, carrying my gear with an enthusiastic smile at the start, then cursing me the entire hike. I try to ignore the heavy weight in my chest and press on with the conversation at hand.

"I don't think you're getting the concept of storm watch for tout le midi." He emphasizes the word midi as if I don't know what locals call this part of the southern France coastline. "Rains are heavy, high winds. My flight was delayed, and now I'm stuck here at a crap two-star hotel in Cannes because the museum gave you all their bloody money."

"I'm going to ignore that remark. Are you getting your news from Millennial tweets again, my friend? Because that could very well be fake news."

"Enough about fake news and all the bloody rest. Old jokes, mate. Get some new material. But seriously. No!" His brows furrow and his tone is forceful. "After you hang up, check your weather app.

"Don't shoot the messenger, Tripp. I'm just telling you the facts. I'm surprised the home owner hasn't called yet. You're high enough on a hill that your rental shouldn't flood, but it's possible flooding could affect many places built on the shore."

"Flooding? How am I supposed to find a supposedly extinct bird in flooding conditions?"

"Thigh high wellies?" Evan chuckles.

"Right. Sure. I brought those here, in my rowboat."

"Excellent!" he says, and I wonder if he's taken me seriously. "Gotta go. I'm trying to find an early morning flight back to Oxford. You take care of yourself, and I'll see you back there soon."

"Oh, I won't be back home for a few weeks, if not more."

"Cor blimey!" He brings his face closer to his camera, so his eyes and nose are all I see on my screen. "Have you not been listening to a word I've said? That island could end up under the Atlantic Ocean, and you're planning on going down all stoic-like, with the locals?"

"It won't be as bad as that, I'm sure, but there's no way home now. May as well find the Skinks-Babbler before the weather takes a turn for the worse."

"You're talking codswallop, but I've known you long enough to realize there's no changing your mind. Just stock up on canned food and water today, will you?"

"Sure, you bet," I shake my head. These weather apps must be mind control in disguise. "Thanks for the info."

Evan gives me a salute, as though I'm a captain going down with my ship, then he ends the call, and the screen goes black. I stare at my phone for a second, just wondering if I should even bother to look at my Accuweather app. There are heavy rains at the moment. I can tell that by looking out the bloody window! I can't be checking my phone every half hour.

My ideal app would be advanced enough to warn me when the weather's taken a turn for the worse, say, a coming tornado, and it would notify me with a ringtone, in a Scottish drawl: "We're doomed, I tell ye, dooooomed!" Sadly, I have yet to find an app like that.

I sit back and try to process the information I just received from Evan. The fire embers are glowing orange; I'll have to go out back to find more dry firewood in the shed, if the temperature keeps dropping, but we'll be fine. Besides a full fridge, we have canned goods and plenty of water. I saw it all in the kitchen pantry earlier this afternoon. I'm sure the rain will be over in a few days, and that flooding is just a worse-case scenario.

"Woof!"

Coffee puts her large paws on my knees, waking me from my daydream.

"Hi? Hi?" It sounds like Jughead's also awake.

Ten

Tripp

"Down, Coffee. Lie down, girl." She obeys. I get up and slowly lift the cover from the bird's cage. He looks up and blinks, then simply stares at me for a few seconds, brilliant, olive-green eyes shining bright. I almost believe that he's going to thank me for turning on the lights.

I open the cage, giving him a cup of my cold, unfinished Earl Grey tea to hold onto. If I familiarize him with some of the sights and smells of this place, he'll be fine here tonight. He grabs at the handle with his claw with a loud tap, tap, tap sound against the china, then dips his big black beak into the tea.

"What the fuck? What the fuck!" He screeches, nodding his head repeatedly while jumping up and down on his perch. I burst out laughing. Did Hannah teach him that?

"It's okay, Jughead. Tea's not your fancy, that's fine, it's fine," I say in a soothing tone. I take out the cup and close the cage. This is going to be your home for a little while," I tell him. He stops jumping and looks over at Coffee, who's on her best behavior, lying on the rug by the fire just staring back.

Once I'm assured both pets are as relaxed as possible, I head upstairs with a new game plan in mind. I'm going to ask Princess Hannah to join me in the field tomorrow.

Will she agree to help me with my gear and research on a rainy forest hike? I highly doubt it. She'll take the easy way out. I'll offer her my truck, she can take the bridge to the mainland and stay in a hotel there. I'll do the hike myself, then take the ferry back in a few days and gather my truck from her then. We'll both get what we want this way: our space.

I tap lightly on the door, and it opens a second later. Hannah is stunning. My breath leaves me and my knees buckle. I'm not even sure how I'm still standing upright.

She's wearing a silky white negligee that fits perfectly across her hips and breasts and highlights her hourglass figure. It has a sheer material, I think it's called organza, framing her breasts all the way up to the bottom of her neck. It leaves much to the imagination, but suddenly, my imagination's working overtime.

"Here. Put this on. It's bloody freezing, and you're half naked." I hand her the white waffle robe that was hanging behind the door and turn away before I can read her expression.

I didn't mean to sound so gruff, but really! Could you have warned me you'd be appearing on my doorstep, catapulting into my life, looking like… that… in the middle of the most important research project of my career?

I was trying to avoid any kind of feelings, but it's a little late for every feeling below the belt. Blast it. I'm buggered.

Hannah says it's fine to turn around, so my hips and legs, which seem to have a mind of their own, pivot me back around. My body is willing; my mind is mushy peas. Of course, she still looks lovely covered up in the white robe, her long ginger hair cascading over her shoulders. Well, this is inconvenient. Didn't think I could go here again. It's been years since I looked at anyone else, thought about anyone else. But, here I am.

I need to get her out of this house before she makes a right hash of everything.

Eleven

Tripp

"Can I come in? We should talk."

I take a step forward, realizing that I've been staring at Hannah far too long. I hope she assumes I'm distracted by the news from my phone call and not that I'm some creepy married scientist. I know my reality, but she doesn't.

I should tell her. I know, I should tell her. I just haven't found the right moment. How do you go from, "Would you like sugar in your tea?" to "My wife died tragically four years ago, and I'm not looking to replace her." I haven't quite figured that one out yet, and none of the pamphlets I was handed in bereavement therapy told me how to handle this situation, either. A waste of perfectly good trees, in my opinion.

She steps to the side, and I walk past her to the French doors that lead to the balcony. I pull open the sheers and look outside to see if anything has improved. Dark, pouring, miserable. We may as well be in bloody Oxford.

"Who was on the phone?" Hannah fluffs several pillows, places them against the hand-carved, sturdy oak headboard, then sits back. She has her phone in her left hand, but she's holding my gaze, and appears not the least bit shy about having me in her room.

"That was Evan, my friend and field technician. He says there won't be any ferry tomorrow. High winds, heavy rain."

"Oh no! This feels more like the Vancouver coast than France. I should have just worked back home."

"I thought the writing wasn't going well back home, and your place is up for sale. So technically, you have no home to go home to."

"Well, yes, I just mean… are you always this argumentative?" She lets out a sigh and pouts. "I mean, bloomin' paltry penguins, okay?"

Her word choice makes me smile, and I try not to chuckle. I'm glad my back is turned to her. "It's just rain." I close the sheers, pull up the desk chair, and sit down. "At least it's not wildfires. Mediterranean France has been devastated by those in the past. Did you look up bird species while I was gone?"

"A few, to pass the time. My best friend, Jillian, isn't answering her Facetime. Speaking of that, I could really use the Wi-Fi password now."

I sigh. May as well give it to her for the night. "Here." I pull out a small piece of paper from my right jeans pocket, walk over to the side of the bed, and hand it to her.

"You wrote it down? Don't you do anything on your phone? You suit your name. You're a real Trip."

"It's William, actually. William Wilson the Third," I explain. "Thanks to the awkward roman letters—triple I's—at the end of my name, the kids at school started calling me Trip. I added the P as a teenager, when every day, some cheeky brat told me I should take a Trip. It got annoying."

"Oops, sorry about that. Kids can be cruel," she says.

"Yes, well, the extra 'p' did nothing to help with the teasing, and then I went into sciences, so I got picked on for being a naff."

"Naff?"

"Incredibly uncool. I still am—I just dress better." I grin.

"It's turned around now. Nerds are considered the best boyfriends. And it's a nice name. It suits you."

What is she doing here? The sexy negligee… buttering me up with compliments… she definitely wants to stay on. I need to scare her away, now. I just got over Mags. I'm not ready for this.

"Yours suits you well, too. Although, I wouldn't say we're in heaven in this particular situation."

"Come on, it's not half bad. We have lights, a fire, and the house is gorgeous. Now, if I could only get uninterrupted service and super-speed Wi-Fi here…" She smirks.

"Ah yes, the bloody Wi-Fi again."

"You think I'm spoiled, I can tell."

"I never said that. It's just socializing with everyone and his uncle isn't at the top of my priority list at the 'mo."

"Oh, you've insinuated that I'm spoiled, from assuming I was an actress from the start to making me get my own dinner after you offered to make it for me."

"If you aren't the pampered Princess, come help me tomorrow in the field. Evan can't make it, there's only you to help me out and limited time before there's too much water in the forest to walk around. I'm on a tight deadline to stake out the area. Besides searching for the Skinks, I plan to build an aviary there."

"An aviary? And you… want me… to be your assistant? Me?"

"I have lots more help, but for the time being, why not? You're a writer. Don't writers seek adventure? It might spark an idea for your screenplay."

"It might spark something like pneumonia! It's cold out there." As if to underline her point, she gets under the white quilt and blankets, pulling them up to her neck.

I knew she wouldn't have the courage to try this with me. Pity, though. I'm not sure what I saw in her, but there was definitely something… more than one something, several things… ah well, now she'll go, and I won't have to worry about whatever this is that I'm feeling.

"Poor Canadian girl. And I thought you Canuck women were strong like moose!"

She glares at me.

"What I do, out there in the wild, it's not for the faint of heart," I continue. "It's fine. It seems that finding this elusive bird simply isn't meant to be my great legacy. I'll pack up my things in the truck tomorrow, and drive you and Jughead across the bridge to Cannes."

Why am I suddenly offering to drive her?

"Hopefully, we can find a hotel to take pity on us and our plight. Unless there are others like us. Let's hope not."

I hear myself invite myself into her life and once again wonder if this is my mother's politeness-gene guiding me, my heart, or something else altogether. Probably a combination of the three.

"Faint of heart… that's what you think of me, Tripp?" Her cheeks have grown rosy pink. It's a sight to see against that red hair. "I'll do it! I'll do it. I'll take you up on your very kind offer. Ever since my crew gave me Jughead, I've always wanted to learn more about rare birds. I'd love to spend the day out in the field with you. Rain, schmain, on the plains in Spain. Let's do this!"

Woah. What a strong-willed woman. I'm taken aback and chuckling at her enthusiasm, or forced enthusiasm, as the case may be, when my phone rings again. This time, it's an ordinary call.

"Wilson here."

Maggie used to tease me that I never knew the word "Hello." Fact is, it's a Waste of Time Word, and yes, I have a list of those.

Now, more than ever, I know that every second counts. Every word. Every breath. Why waste one? You say hello, the other person asks who's speaking. Instead, just cut to the chase, tell them who's answering the damn phone, and they'll get to the matter at hand. Maggie always said, "Silly, sensible scientist," when I explained that. I miss her so.

"Mr. Wilson. Sorry to disturb, it's James, the owner. I'm in Florida, on holiday. Just got word that there's flooding around the island? Neighbor tells me the ferries stopped running, and the Valois bridge was closed a half hour ago. They're concerned it may give way."

"That bridge on the other side of the island? But then there's no way back to the mainland…" I stand up and look out the window. It's pitch black out there, and the rain's still pouring down in buckets, but I don't hear any high winds. I don't see what the fuss is about, it's just water. People look at the weather apps these days and cancel their plans when it says two percent chance of snow. It's bloody ridiculous.

"Well, that's the least of our problems. Did you hear about the Good Nights mix up? The blasted app booked in another woman with me, same dates. She's here with me now. Seems we're stuck here, with the bridge closed."

"What? Unbelievable. I'm so sorry, I didn't know. I'll get in touch with Good Nights, make sure they reimburse you both. My neighbor wants to come over with some food and water for you, since stores will be closed a few days. Béatrice is supposed to come by sometime tomorrow, not sure if she still will. She's in a house on other side of the island, right on the shore, actually..."

"Yes, she already cleaned once, the other day. She's lovely. We have enough food. We'll be fine, it's just a little rain. And the house is beautiful."

"Okay... well, I'll be in touch again soon."

I don't think he expected me to be so easy-going about all of this, but bloody hell, it's just rain. A lot of rain. It's not like it's a tsunami. He ends the call, and I put my phone to sleep, then look over at Hannah. She's fallen asleep. She's luminous, her hair spread out like a mermaid's locks, painting the white bedcover red. She has three adorable freckles on her dainty nose and extremely long, black eyelashes. Even the way she curls one hand under her face… so sweet.

Now, she's going to have to stay. There's no way to get her to the mainland. I'm surprised to find that I like being in her company. Pleasantly surprised.

Stop this! She's funny and interesting, a bit entitled, perhaps, but either way, I didn't plan on company. Attractive, adventurous company at that. I don't need any distractions while working. In fact, I don't need female distraction, ever again. I'm done. Finished. Heart closed for business, thank you and goodnight.

She said yes. She said she'd join me in the field, even before she learned the bridge was out and we were stranded here. Unbelievable, really, how we can make assumptions about a person and be way off base. Mind, I don't actually know what she's made of, yet. I have no idea how she'll do out there, especially in these conditions. She may end up cursing me all the way home, like Maggie did.

Maggie. Oh, Mags. What am I even thinking? I'm not. This isn't thinking. It's feeling, and it's not for me. Been there, done that, and the t-shirt is burning in hell.

I take one last look at the sleeping Princess, then walk out of the room, leaving the door slightly ajar.

Rain or no rain, Hannah or no Hannah, I'll set out first thing tomorrow morning.

Twelve

Hannah

I'm standing by the front door, dressed and ready to go in a glossy, bright blue rain coat and white running shoes. It's all I packed for colder weather, and the raincoat is definitely one of those purchases I would put in the 'regret later' category. I feel like a fresh, plump blueberry. I am not winning any fashion awards today, so this getup had better keep me dry.

The living room air is filled with the delectable aroma of freshly brewed coffee, eggs, and toast. I only ate a few more crumpets last night, so I'm famished, and the mingling scents are making me salivate.

I don't want to assume this meal is for me, though. I can grab something on the road if he doesn't invite me. I need to prove to Tripp that I'm a self-sufficient woman. After our battle of wits over this rental, and perhaps because I'm an unemployed writer vacationing in France, he seems to think I'm some kind of spoiled celebrity brat.

Well, sure. I like things how I like them. I enjoy warm food and a hot bath when I can get one. I'm no Anne LaBastille, but don't tell me I can't handle a walk in the woods!

Tripp thinks I can't cope for one day out in the field searching for a little bird? That I don't have what it takes? I've put up with sexism in the workplace, trying to break through the glass ceiling in high heels and a shatterproof industry roof, being sexually harassed by one of my bosses on a plane ride—talk about being cornered, I went and hung out with an airline assistant most of the flight because she was someone who 'got it'—and the leering, whistling and, if it was an exceptionally bad day, gyrating that every woman has to endure the minute she walks out her front door wearing anything attractive. I don't care how cliché it sounds, it's true: it's a jungle out there. We have to put on protective mental gear and ass-kicking boots for every step we take.

He wants to see some endurance? I've got that. Street smarts? Ha. I could play soccer on the streets of L.A., shoot hoops in downtown Vancouver. Surely, birding takes the same kind of stamina. I'll show him. Besides, I wasn't able to write one word again this morning. Not one good one, anyway. Hopefully, by saying yes to this adventure, I'll be able to kick-start my writing, too.

"C'mere girl! Come to Daddy!"

Tripp comes fast around the corner, with the other Coffee in his life trailing behind him, tail wagging, obviously excited to get outside. He told me the forest is about half an hour from here, and I'm sure she can't wait that long until we make it to the field.

"I'm not sure how I feel about being whistled for, but the Daddy thing is kinda hot," I say in my best vacant, southern-gal type drawl. I smirk at him as I lean back against the glass.

Tripp chuckles and looks down at his dog. It seems that he's trying to avoid eye contact. "Well, you're in a good mood and up bright and early, ready to go! Nice slicker."

At least he didn't call me a blueberry. Yet. "I slept well after a hot bath late last night. I was up before you, texting my mom, feeding Jughead, and cleaning his cage. I didn't want to delay you this morning." I bend down to meet Coffee and give her ears and head a rub.

"You're still joining me?" His eyes meet mine. He looks torn.

"Sure! Sounds like an adventure. Then, once we find your bird, as long as the bridge reopens, you can leave and let me have the place all to myself, right? I mean there would be no reason for you to stay on, and you can just return on the credit that Good Nights is bound to offer us both after this disaster."

"So, you heard about the bridge? Before you fell asleep last night…" Interesting, how he's conveniently ignoring that last part and instead focusing on the flood.

"Yes. I heard and physically and mentally gave up trying to figure out what to do next. I decided my next move was sleep."

"Good decision. But I'm not as sure about this one. You want to trek through a possibly flooded forest with me instead of staying in this luxurious villa? I didn't take you for the adventurous type..."

"I'm here, aren't I? I came all the way from Burnaby."

"For a solo writer's retreat, Hannah. Not in the name of serious science."

"Look," I cross my arms, "I am serious! You said you needed help. I've graciously offered it. Do you want my help, or don't you?"

He looks me up and down for a moment, then exhales. I can't decipher what the sigh means.

"Let's give it a whirl and pray the birds aren't frightened out of their feathers by that slicker. Help yourself to some eggs and coffee. We'll leave in fifteen." He says it sternly, as though he's proposing a business deal.

"The coffee smells great, but I thought you only drank tea?"

"No, I drink both. Could have done with something much stronger this morning."

He looks right over my head, then before I can say anything more, he slides past and opens the front door for Coffee, following swiftly behind her as she bounds down the driveway.

Thirteen

Hannah

"Here. There will be lots of mud puddles. You're going to need these." Tripp reaches back to the narrow backseat of his truck, gives his gleeful dog a pat, digs around a little, then hands me a pair of glossy, army green rain boots.

"Water boots—we call them wellies. They were Maggie's. I think they'll fit you."

"Maggie? Who's Maggie?"

He turns and stares at me for thirty seconds, saying nothing. It's as though he's deciding if he can trust me with delicate information.

"My late wife."

The air feels very close inside this truck. "Oh, I'm so sorry. I-I didn't mean to pry." I hear myself stutter a little and feel my heart beating faster inside my chest. When we first met, I thought he was a workaholic who'd abandoned his wife so he could do research alone. Later, I just thought he'd left her, like Doug left me. I'm angry at myself for being so quick to judge this man.

"Don't be," he says softly and switches his gaze away from me to look out the window. "Back in Oxford, I wasn't sure why I was bringing the wellies on this trip. For some strange reason, I felt compelled to throw them in my duffel bag, along with my camouflage ones. Now, I know why."

I look down at the "wellies." I hate the dull rain boot color, but realize we can't go around in bright colors, scaring away all the birds, especially since Tripp already hinted that my raincoat is a project liability. I open the truck door, sit on the edge of the seat, and try to pull on the right boot. I didn't realize what a struggle putting on a boot this way would be. Oh no, no-no-no-no, I'm going to fall and wreck my faaaaace!

"Limey lorikeets!"

I promised myself to get creative with my cursing, but limey? I've turned into a wacky, British teenage girl around this man.

I've completely lost my balance, and I'm about to fall face-first onto the wet gravel road when Tripp appears in front of me, grabbing me firmly at the waist.

"Love that you made the Lorikeets British, Hannah. Well done."

We're so close, I feel his warm breath on my collar bone. He hoists me back into the seat, gives the boot that's halfway on my foot a little shove, and it slides on perfectly. He takes the left boot from the truck floor, places it like a trophy on his open palm, and looks up at me.

"You're the eighteenth maiden we've tried, in all the land," he says it like a proper, royal Englishman. "This boot bloody well better fit."

"Oh, it will. I locked up every other bitch in the basement," I say without a trace of a smile.

He laughs so hard, the sound echoes across the field. After placing the boot on my foot, he offers up his right hand and helps me down and out of the truck.

I sweep several messy strands of hair away from my eyes and take a look around. It's serene here at the forest's edge. There are no other people or parked cars or oncoming traffic, just rows and rows of coniferous trees. I can hear crickets chirping in the tall grass, the whistling wind, a light drizzle of rain.

I look up at Tripp and realize that I'm still holding his hand, and we're staring at each other in complete silence. He has a strong, chiseled chin and very full lips framed by that sexy bit of red and brown stubble. I didn't think I liked beards, but his looks like a properly kept, four-day growth, not the longer I'm-a-lazy-slob-and-I-don't-wanna-shave look. I've worked in television and met many celebrities, but I've never looked in the eyes of a man this achingly gorgeous. I keep staring, forgetting why we're even here.

"Now, the hard work starts." Tripp abruptly drops my hand and turns to get Coffee out of the truck. It's great that he loves his dog, but a part of me wants to hit him on the head with some ornithology equipment. Way to break the mood, grumpy crumpet.

"You may want to tie your hair back. It's quite windy," he calls over his shoulder.

I have an elastic hairband around my wrist, so I tie back my tresses while he's pulling bags out from under a tarp in the cab of his truck.

"Are you sure it's going to be safe in there?" I bend down and give Coffee a rub. She's sitting at her master's feet, gazing into the forest, whimpering as she waits for the golden go-ahead sign.

"Safe? Sure, we're nowhere near the shore or any flooding rivers, and the worst of the rain has passed over. But, I'm warning you, it's not going to be pleasant," he says, handing me a backpack as he puts on his own. He looks right at me. "You still in?"

"I'm still in," I say, wondering what exactly I'm getting myself into.

Fourteen

Tripp

We've walked three-and-a-half kilometers and are nearing the part of the forest where I plan to drop the nylon mist nets. If I can capture and photograph the Skinks Babbler, which has been elusive to all and believed extinct for more than seventy-five years, I'll get my place in the history books.

The rows of tall pine trees have managed to break the wind quite a bit, but the rain is starting to soak through my jacket. I wonder how miserable my new research assistant feels in her borrowed boots and thin, blue slicker.

Hannah is keeping the pace with me, and I have yet to hear one complaint, despite the gentle slope we're climbing, the blowing wind, and the driving rain. I was wrong about her. It sounds like she's had an interesting career in entertainment, but she hasn't been spoon-fed all her life, or, if she has, she's certainly making up for lost time now.

"We're here!"

"This is where you want to set up? Okay, so I've got the pole-thingies you'll use to put up the nets, and you've got the nets and the camera?"

"And binoculars, yes. I'm sure it's all getting rather heavy for you. Let's take a lunch break first, there, in the underbrush, by that log. Have a seat."

I help her take off her backpack and place it along with mine on the tarp I've set up on the ground. She sits down on the tarp under the canopy of trees, opens her water bottle, takes a swig, then looks around.

"It's so peaceful."

"It is. I love this forest. But, I like quiet. I don't often have music on in the house, and I'm not big on television anymore, no offense to your profession."

"None taken. I'd write stage plays if there were any money in it."

"Really? Thought it was a bit of a dying art for our generation."

"Not for me. I did theatre studies in university. I love writing for a live audience. There's a beautiful sense of teamwork in a theatrical production. Television, well, it's more and more about the ratings. There are even shows built around commercials!"

"And those are mostly drug commercials," I say.

"Yes! So annoying." She nods, pulls part of her shirt up from under her slicker, and wipes her face. It is pouring out here. She's being a sport.

"Eighty percent of those commercials are taken up with some deep authoritative voice telling you the ailments you could get, which are all worse than if you just didn't take the bloody drug: Be careful," I say, my voice low. "You may grow an extra limb… or penis…"

"Exactly!" Hannah's laughing so hard, tears are starting to form in the outside creases of her eyes. She was so uptight when we first met. I love making her laugh.

"And they all speak like auctioneers who've had one too many espressos. It always makes me wonder, if I take the drug, is that what I'm gonna sound like? Because thanks, I'll just stick with my heart condition…"

"You have a heart condition?"

"No, you naff. I don't have a heart condition."

She smiles up at me.

Aw. I can get away with calling her a naff. Lovely.

"Okay, that's good, because I wouldn't want to over excite you."

"You're going to over excite me?"

She just bites her lower lip. I'd better change the subject.

"I'm sorry about the rain. The forecast said the worst had already come."

"Not exactly what I expected for a south of France vacation." She chuckles, pulls her hood tighter over her head, and wipes some raindrops off her nose.

"Mother Nature is full of surprises. Like with this bird. I know it's out here. I just need to use the element of surprise. Catch it when it's out looking for food."

"You'll let it go after, right? The nets are safe for the birds?"

I crouch down and sit beside her. "I wouldn't have it any other way. They're commonplace now, after a bit of a controversy at the start. They're perfectly safe if you use them correctly, and I'll only be tagging the Skinks so we can locate it again. I'll let it go as soon as I get its age, sex, weight, and photograph it."

"Can that all happen today?" She rummages through one of the lunch bags I prepared and hands me a sandwich, then takes one for herself.

"I'm not so sure." I take a longer look around, glancing up at the darkening skies. "I'm not keen to put up the nets if I can't return tomorrow morning to take them down. That wouldn't be fair to the Skinks at all."

She studies me quietly, then takes another sip of water. "You really care about this bird. What's the fascination?"

She looks like a little wet bluebird in the rain, her knees scrunched up to her chest in an attempt to get warm. I feel the sudden urge to wipe the rain drops off her eyelids, to kiss that freckled nose. I have to look away.

"I suppose it started with my father," I say, handing her a thermos of hot chocolate she didn't know I'd packed. Her eyes sparkle with gratitude.

"He was in the same field. He wanted to find the Skinks, too, and it became an obsession of sorts. He once said that birds thought extinct and then found are a little like ghosts, appearing, then disappearing. They're mystical."

"So, we're like ghostbusters." She chuckles.

"Maybe. Hopefully we won't come out of this completely covered in marshmallow goo."

That makes her laugh out loud, and I adore the sound. We eat and drink in silence for a moment. Then, she speaks softly. "My Dad died when I was very young. You're lucky you had him."

"Oh, that's awful." I look down, not knowing what else to say. Then, suddenly, I do. "I didn't really have him, though. That's the thing. I never could compete with his damn work. I remember pouring through his bird books up in his office, learning about hundreds of elusive species while he did his research at his desk. I wanted to impress him. It was all for naught."

"Didn't he ever take you out birding?"

"Never. Not once. He was very serious about this work. Said it wasn't child's play."

"Oh, that's not… not so nice. I'm sorry."

"You say sorry a lot."

"I do? Sorry!" She scrunches up her nose.

I look at her again and chuckle. "Stop apologizing. It's not your fault my parents had icicle hearts."

"Ouch! That bad?" She's warming her hands on the thermos cup now.

"They say it's never too late to have a happy childhood. I suppose I'm having mine now." I smile at her and raise my cup. She clinks hers with mine.

"To a happy childhood, this time around, then," she says. "And to finding your Skinks Babbler!"

I notice she can't say the term without smirking. "Yes, well, I hope this outing proves useful for your screenplay."

"Hmm," she sips her drink, then puts it down. "I write romantic comedy. This day has been more like a documentary."

I study her face: rosy cheeks, a wet strand of ginger hair matted against her left cheek, and start to speak, but I can't get the words out. I can't say what I want to. I can't say, "It could be romantic." Why am I even thinking of her in this way? I love how I feel around her, but I'm in awe of it all.

I glance up at the sky again, searching for the right words. The clouds are dark and menacing. I don't like what I see or hear. That was thunder.

"Bugger. It's a comedy of sorts. I'm supposed to be showing you how to capture a rare bird, but instead, we're running from a nasty storm." I stand up.

"What?" Hannah stands and looks up at the sky, too.

"I'm sorry."

"Now you're apologizing!"

"Well," I say, gathering up the thermoses and tarp, shoving everything into its pack, "I have to because I told you it would be safe." I regret telling her that. If this is anything more than a rain storm; if Hannah gets hurt in this, I'll never forgive myself.

"It's... it's not safe?" She wraps her arms around herself for a moment, looking panicked.

I put my hands on her shoulders and look her in the eyes. "Hannah. It's going to be okay. I'll take care of you. But we have to move fast."

I sling a backpack over each shoulder, motion for Coffee to follow us, grab Hannah's hand, and lead the way.

Fifteen

Hannah

"We're almost there," Tripp calls over his shoulder, gently pulling my left hand as we make our way down the slippery, muddy path. My forehead and eyelids are completely soaked with raindrops, so I'm thankful that he's leading the way. His skin on mine is warm and reassuring.

As a Canadian, I've grown accustomed to storms. I've shoveled driveways into snowbanks far taller than my five-feet five-inches. I've also lived under rainy, grey skies for months, and even taken a few walks in stormy weather out on the beach.

This is no ordinary storm. The skies have turned as black as night, the wind makes eerie squeals through the trees, and the rain is relentless. I'm not sure what type of storm it is, so I'm going to call it Category Get My Ass Outta Here.

I take my free hand and wipe my eyes, sweeping away a few strands of wet hair at the same time. Now I can see a speck of light in the distance, where these rows of trees stop, and we can enter an open field. I'm not sure that will be an improvement, however, since the trees must be breaking these high winds a little.

Tripp starts down the final slope, not far from where he parked the truck. He turns to face me and starts to take my other hand to help me down. He's one second too late.

"Wanking warblers!" My, that was elegant.

Tripp isn't laughing, but it's not because of my word choice. "Don't move!" he shouts.

I'm lying in the mud on my stomach. I've banged my knee up badly, and I try to push myself up, but before I succeed, Tripp's at my side, rolling me just a little so he can inspect my leg.

"Hannah, you're bleeding, Oh God… I'm so sorry." He's more serious than I've ever seen him. He lifts my pant leg and carefully examines my knee. It feels like I've just had knee surgery, but I know it's just a cut. I don't get why he's pale and silent all of a sudden.

"So much blood," he says.

"I'm fine. It's nothing," I try to reassure him. Isn't it supposed to be the other way around? He's not panicked, but he's definitely not EMS material. Good thing he's sexy in every other way.

"It's deep, but I can fix this. I have a first aid kit in the truck. Come on, put your arms around my neck, I'll lift you the rest of the way."

I cling to him as he carries me out of the forest, onto a path surrounded by tall, golden grass. It's so windy, I have to bury my head into his neck. That's when I hear him mumbling.

"It said storm warning, but I ignored it. I thought the worst was over. Shouldn't have let my guard down."

I've never seen this side of him. He's acting like a soldier in battle.

"Let your guard down?" I lift my head to speak. "Tripp, it's just weather. It's unpredictable. It flooded so much already, we thought the heavy rain was over."

"I promised to keep you safe."

His voice cracks on "safe," and I'm so moved by the emotion in his voice, I don't know what to answer. I bury my head back into his neck, praying the storm will pass soon.

Tripp opens the door, and Coffee scurries inside and shakes herself off immediately. Neither of us bother to scold her because we're both soaking wet anyway.

"Couch okay?" Tripp asks, and I nod. He carries me over to living room couch and places me down. It's such a cozy spot. I take off my rain coat and sling it over the chair beside the couch. He gently pulls off my boots, then his, then gathers everything and hangs it up as I settle myself.

"I don't think we need a fire tonight. It's warmer."

"Yes, must be a tropical storm. Those winds were over one hundred kilometers an hour. I hope everyone along the shore is okay. Bridge will be staying out." Tripp runs his hands through his wet hair and glances over at Jughead, who is bopping up and down, making a bit of a fuss in his cage. He sits down at the edge of the couch by my feet, adjusting the pillow under my injured knee.

"I'll feed Coffee and Jughead. What do you want to eat?"

"Oh, no. No. I'm not your patient. Like I said, just a bruise and minor cut." I glance down at my bandaged knee. It really does hurt, but I don't want him going back to thinking I'm a spoiled Canadian brat. I'm a grown woman, and I can manage to make my own meals.

I would love some of his delicious tea though. I smile to myself. I actually mean tea. Although…

"We'll see about that. I'll start with a pot of Earl Grey, yes?" he says.

He read my mind.

"And you'll need anti-inflammatories. A towel for your hair. And dry clothes. I'll be right back." He's calmer now than he was out in the forest. I suppose he just isn't keen on the sight of blood. He did everything right to treat the wound and get me back here, but he didn't seem to really be with me, to be present. It was like his mind was elsewhere the whole time.

Tripp walks into the room slowly, and I can hear the tray of teacups clinking against each other. For a moment he just stops in his tracks beside the couch, then sets it down on the coffee table. I notice him watching me but keep pretending that I'm reading my phone. I can feel his eyes on me still and feel compelled to look up and meet his gaze.

"Hey, you," he says. "I've got drugs."

"I'm glad, because I can't reach my usual dealer. There's no service."

"What?" He bends down and looks at my phone. "Bloody hell. We're living in the dark ages. I could turn on the television…"

"Nah," I interrupt. Funny, I don't really care about the outside world right now. "We have solid windows and doors, right? All that matters." I lean over and start to grab the teapot, but he takes it from me.

"Sit back. Rest. It's not a tornado, if that's what you're wondering," Tripp says as he pours two cups of tea. "I had to learn about weather patterns for my work. It's a severe thunderstorm, high winds, heavy rains, but, my dear, we wouldn't be here right now if that was a tornado chasing the truck."

My dear. That's so old school for someone our age, but I love how it sounds. He's delicious, and I think he finally likes me.

I settle back against the pillow Tripp brought me, take a sip of warm tea, and swallow the painkillers. My knee isn't throbbing as much anymore, but I have a happy heart. Maybe that's why.

Tripp passes me my favorite pair of loose yoga pants and a grey sweatshirt. "Thought you may not want to climb the stairs just yet. Change into those. I'll be in the kitchen making you that dinner I reneged on earlier. A day in the field like this, you deserve it."

Oh, my. A man who admits his mistakes and cooks. I can't believe I didn't want to share this space with him at first. I've found my Utopia.

And… I have an idea for a screenplay! If I could only concentrate on writing it, instead of daydreaming about how muscular Tripp's ass looks in those worn blue jeans.

"Bloody 'el," Jughead squawks.

Sixteen

Tripp

"Behold, I bring you light and ice. It's not my fault about the rain, or the infinite darkness. Should you decide to board Noah's Ark, please be sure to leave this fine establishment an online review first."

Hannah looks up at me and chuckles. I'm holding up an old glass kerosene lamp that I found inside the dining room cabinet. I set it down on the coffee table, then pass her the ice I've wrapped in a dish towel.

"Thanks." She smiles and places the towel on her knee. "I had a feeling the power would go out tonight, but I didn't expect you to be able to finish cooking in there. That was pure entertainment, hearing the pots clinging and clanging and you cursing away… exotic bird names only, of course," she teases.

"Luckily, it was already cooked when the blackout happened—I just had to serve it up. I've got it all set out in the dining room for us. Do you think you can hobble on over there?"

I sit on the couch at the empty spot by her feet. They're covered by the plaid blanket I gave her, her knee resting on the pillow. Hannah is using her cell flashlight. It looks like she's been writing something on her phone. Why didn't I think of that, instead of bumping around in the pitch-black kitchen, cursing like a sailor the entire time?

"Tripp, I'm only raising and icing it because you told me so. It's fine. It's just bruised. I'm sure it will be better by tomorrow." She starts to sit up, keeping the ice pack firm against her knee. "Tofu toucans! That hurts!"

I chuckle, but then notice how pink her face has grown and put my hand on her knee to stabilize it, not realizing her hand is already there. Our hands remain touching in the silence. She's not taking hers away.

It's both of us, then. We both feel it. Bugger. I have to tell her about the cursing thing, before it goes on for too long. I'm going to have to use the steaks I cooked as blackmail here. Otherwise, she may never speak to me again.

"Stop being a heroine," I break the silence, picking her up in my arms. "Just let me help you." I bend down to grab the kerosene lamp to light my way, then set off slowly to the dining room.

"Now, this is what I call service. That online review, Sir, is nearing five stars."

"It may well not be when I tell you what I'm about to tell you," I say softly as we near the dining room table. "Please remember I'm just a lowly scientist who likes a good laugh, especially when it's at the expense of a beautiful, Canadian gal with a good sense of humor… I hope…"

"What good laugh?" She blinks up at me in the darkness, her face aglow only by the lamp. She looks stunning. "Tell me!"

We've reached the table. I place the kerosene lamp at the center, along with a second one I found in the cabinet earlier. They cast a low light across the length of the rectangular table. Our meals are set out across from each other at the far end, decorated with good silver, red linen napkins, and the gold rimmed wine glasses I found in the cabinet.

"Oh, my goodness, you did all of this?"

"You like it? Okay, that's good." I help her sit down, making sure her ice pack stays on her knee, then gently push the chair in.

"Like it? Tripp, this is incredible!"

I walk around the table and sit opposite her. She's looking down, admiring her side garden salad and everything on her plate: steak, carrots, and mashed potatoes garnished with parsley. There are several strong aromas mingling across the table: melted butter, mushrooms sautéed with olive oil and garlic, kerosene oil burning in the lamps. I hate to admit it, but I'm rather glad that the lights went out.

This is the first time in four years that I've sat down to enjoy a meal with a woman.

Don't overthink this or you'll hyperventilate and pass out!

The lamp light was necessary, but it sets a lovely mood.

"So," I say, trying to clear my mind of any more damaging, or arousing, thoughts. "Would you like a glass of red?"

She nods, and I pour her some red wine from the carafe, and then a glass for myself.

"Here's the thing." I wait until she has taken a full sip of wine and swallowed it. "I never read a book by a psychologist about using bird names for swearing."

She looks at me and sets down her glass. "You made it up?"

"Yeah. I made the whole thing up. I was just messing with you." I give her a sheepish smile, raising one eyebrow. Should I duck? Get up from the table and hide?

"Tripp!" She glares at me for a second, then starts laughing uncontrollably. "You made me say limey lorikeets! You made me wrack my brain for ridiculous word combinations!" she says through bits of laughter.

"I did do that, yes, indeed." I grin. "I couldn't help myself—you were such an easy target!"

She picks up her red napkin and tosses it at my head. "You're a wankpuffin!"

I take the napkin off my head and set it aside. I'm laughing so hard, I have tears starting to stream out of the corners of my eyes.

"The best part was watching your face when you came up with using 'tofu' and 'toucans' together. Except, you were hurting, and I don't like that, so that's when I decided maybe I should tell you."

Her laughter is easing now. She's taking another sip of wine and still smiling at me with her eyes. Looks like I don't have to run for cover. Perhaps I'm better at interacting with women than I thought. I was sure I was going to balls this up.

"You got me good! And then you cooked all of this for me. So, I won't hold a grudge, but you'd better watch your back. I can execute a great practical joke as good as any British chap."

"You can?"

"No, not really, but I'll work on it." She starts cutting her steak. "That's what this trip was all about. Trying new things. Not saying no to experiences as often as I had been."

"So far, you've lived with a stranger in a foreign country, stopped dropping the F-bomb, worked as a field assistant for an ornithologist, trekked in a severe thunderstorm…"

"And now I'm having a fancy dinner in the dark. Go figure. I've never done that, either."

"I have to admit, I thought you were a spoiled, selfish Canadian princess when we first met, and here you are, eating by a kerosene lamp, and you haven't complained that the Wi-Fi is down once." I mince no words. I need to see her reaction.

"Oh my God," she whines emphatically, "the Wi-Fi's down?"

I'm quite sure she's kidding but am relieved when she gives me a cheeky grin.

"Maybe I have that side of me, yes, but there's more to me than meets the eye, like anyone. People are like onions. You have to deal with the fumes at first and peel back the layers."

"Fumes? Are you saying I stink?" I chuckle.

"You reeked of arrogance when we met, that's for sure," she says. "But I peeled back the layers and found kindness and humor and brilliance."

"So, clearly, I have reasons to be arrogant."

"Stop." She smirks. "You'll spoil the mood."

We finish our meal in comfortable silence. It's lovely that we can sit here, sharing a meal by the light of kerosene lamps. I'm sitting with someone who was a stranger, someone I wanted out of here only twenty-four hours ago, and now, she feels like my friend. And I hope that she'll stay as long as she wants.

Seventeen

Tripp

Once we're finished eating, we leave the dishes on the table to deal with later, and I carry her back to the couch. The power still hasn't returned, so we have the two kerosene lamps on the coffee table, along with the carafe of wine and our empty glasses. She's sitting with her leg propped up on the pillow, and I'm sitting opposite her, legs up as well. Coffee is asleep by my recliner, and Jughead is unusually quiet, so he must be napping.

"Are you cold?" I grab the blanket that fell to the floor and pull it over the both of us.

"Not now," she says sleepily. "This is cozy. Delicious food, great company. Five-star vacation. Maybe not the hot one I anticipated…"

I dare not tell her how hot it feels to me, how my body and heart are feeling that good ache I haven't felt in ages. Not yet. She's told me so much about herself, and I've held back. I know she didn't understand my reaction to her getting hurt in the storm. I need to explain to her, now. I should try. I won't know if I don't try.

"It isn't just you, you know. I haven't been good at trying anything new for a very long time, either," I say, reaching over and pouring her some wine. "There was a time that I didn't even want to live."

Hannah is unusually silent, so I continue.

"My wife was killed in the London subway bombing four years ago."

I can't see her face in this low lighting, but I can hear her gasp lightly. "Oh my God. I-I don't have words. Do you want to talk about it?"

"Yes. Couldn't for years, but I can now."

"Were you with her?"

"No, I wasn't. I wish I was. Maybe, somehow, I could have saved her."

"That's what… that's why you were panicked in the forest with me today. You were…"

"Yeah, maybe. Maybe." I sigh. "I was reliving it all a little. I still do that from time to time."

"It's okay. I'm fine."

I can hear her taking a swig of wine and decide that I desperately need to do the same. I take a full swallow and a deep breath before speaking again.

"The day of the bombing, I was at the museum leading a group of students around, when mass pandemonium broke out. People were screaming and running for the exits. Someone said there'd been an explosion in the subway. I checked my phone. Maggie hadn't messaged, and I assumed she'd already made it to work.

"But as the hours went by, that nagging feeling that she had been in the underground at the time of the explosion grew stronger and stronger. When it was deemed safe for us to return to home, I walked back to our apartment with a few colleagues. They had all heard from their spouses by then. Evan, who lives in the building across the street, offered to stay with me, just until there was word either way. He was the one who picked up the call from Maggie's office—I was in the kitchen trying to make us something to eat. She had never arrived for work that day."

"Tripp…"

"It's strange. We wake up, eat a fast breakfast, rush out the door to work, maybe we peck our spouses on the lips, maybe we don't have time… I don't even remember our last goodbye. I wish I could remember what we said to each other. I wish I could remember the sound of her voice, her scent. So much of that fades away."

I suddenly realize I'm going on about intimate details, things Hannah wouldn't understand, or wouldn't want to hear. I start to get up from the couch, but she reaches out and takes both my hands in hers, pulling me back down, closer to her.

"You can keep talking, you know. It's fine, and it may help."

I gaze out the window and think about how drastically my life changed after the bombing. Besides the constant ache of missing Mags and the monotony of drifting about our lonely apartment like the walking dead, for the longest time, I was afraid to venture out as far as the corner store. I was afraid to live. Not a day went by when I wasn't thinking about terrorists and bombings and who they might hurt next. Therapy eventually helped me manage my fear, but it couldn't bring back my wife. Words can't resurrect our lives, only actions can do that.

I finally came to the island when I'd had enough of staring at our photographs on the living room wall. I couldn't bear to take them down, but I also couldn't take seeing those memories every hour of every day. Everything in the apartment reminded me of her. Here, in this house, out in the woods, I've found a kind of haven. I don't find her in everything I see or touch anymore, but there's still a place for her in my heart as I go about my day.

Suddenly, I remember I'm speaking with Hannah. I've probably been staring into space far too long. "I saw a therapist for a while. Didn't really help. They said time would heal, but it's four years on, and I still miss her."

"Don't you think that's normal? Don't you think you'll always miss her?" She pauses for a moment, then continues. "I lost my dad when I was just six. I still think about him every day. I still miss him. Every day. It never goes away, Tripp. You just find ways to deal with the pain over time. You find more and more ways, so it becomes a bit easier. But it never goes away."

"You're one of the first people to be honest with me about grief." I give her hand a squeeze. "Thank you."

"Just being real. You're welcome." She shifts her weight and lets out a sigh. "I have a confession," she says. "I wanted this place all to myself, but now, I'm glad we're here together."

I want to do more than hold her hands. I want to crawl under this blanket, come up for air on the other end, and kiss her like she's never been kissed before.

But, I have to resist. She needs time to digest what I've told her, and I need time to be certain it's not just the warm food, low light, and red wine that's making me feel drunk on love.

"So," I stand up, slowly, then turn away from her, bending to give Coffee a pat.

"Everything in the freezer's going to melt soon. Sundaes by kerosene lamp? What do you say?"

"I never say no to ice cream."

I turn to go make the sundaes, but suddenly, she's standing, preparing, I assume, to make her way to the kitchen to help me. She holds my arm for stability and balance; I wrap it around my neck and support most of her weight as she hobbles along.

"Tripp?" I hear her ask me softly in the darkness.

"Yeah?"

"This has been an unexpectedly good night," she whispers. "Maybe the app name is perfect, after all."

There's that good ache again.

Eighteen

Hannah

The lanky girl at the front door has a toothy smile, soaking wet hair, and a pail full of cleaning supplies.

I wasn't sure what to expect when the doorbell rang early this morning. Maybe people from BC Hydro coming to fix the fallen power lines? Then, as I groggily made my way down the stairs, one at a time on my behind like a toddler in diapers often does to save my aching knee, I remembered where I am, who I'm with, and our evening last night. My cheeks flushed, recalling the romantic feelings that stirred inside me, but when I opened the door, a gust of wind and driving rain changed all that.

"Come in. Please, come in!" I let the teenager inside, taking her pail from her left hand. She's left standing there with a mop, her tightly-curled, raven-black hair dripping wet.

"I am cleaner, Béatrice," she says. Her big, brown eyes captivate my attention first, then her strong French accent.

"Oh my! You came in this storm? But the power is out…" I take her thin raincoat and hang it on the brass hook beside the door.

"No, no. You're not cleaning today, Béatrice, *asseyons-nous, pour du thé*," Tripp, has come up behind us with a large tray of tea and crumpets. How did he manage to heat the water? He's already dressed in dark blue jeans and a maroon t-shirt, the obvious early-riser in this household compared to me, still in my pink I NEED MY BEAUTY SLEEP nightshirt. He ushers the girl to have breakfast with us in the living room.

"How's the knee this morning?" He glances up at me as he places a small china sugar bowl and an elegant china creamer on the coffee table. I take a seat beside Béatrice on the couch as he passes me my Earl Grey, already stirred, exactly how I like it.

"It's fine. Sore kneecap, but fine otherwise. Enough about me. Why did this poor girl feel she had to come and work here in the storm?"

"It's my only job. I need it," I hear her say firmly, and when I turn to her, I see fear in her eyes.

I look away, taken aback. I've never felt what I see in her eyes in my life. I'm trying to come up with a screenplay to sell so I can get my writing career back on track, but I know I have a backup plan if that goes awry. My mom will lend me money, or I'll get a smaller condo, or I could take some contract business writing work for a while. This girl doesn't look like she has options. She looks malnourished, tired, and alone. What's her story?

As she stirs cream into her tea, Tripp hands her a plate of crumpets with jam, then sits back in what I'm now coming to think of as "his" recliner. "We still have no power, but I used my camping BioEase Kettlepot to boil the water. I even warmed the crumpets in there.

Ah, so that's how he did it. He is such an adept scientist, chef, and woodsman. Remind me to always take him with me in a crisis.

Holy three-sixty, Hannah! I've come a long way from trying to manipulate and kick him out of this place! Mom was right: the heart knows what it wants and best of luck to any brain that gets in its way.

"Béatrice and I met once before." Tripp looks at me, reaches down to give his loyal friend Coffee a chin scratch, and then, as though reading my mind, proceeds to answer all of my questions about our house guest. "I practiced my French with her. I was a little rough around the edges, because it's been a while since I've spoken it, but a little English from her, a few French words from me… we managed to make it work.

"She's from the *Côte d'Ivoire* and came here to work with her mother when she was eleven. They fled their country at the height of the civil war there, but soon after, her mother died of kidney disease. Béatrice somehow managed to hide from social services, stayed in her house along the shore, and found work with the tourists. She's been unemployed for a while but got this job at the start of this year.

"She's very sweet, and she said she's doing fine, but I'm concerned about her," he says. "She came to clean just the other day. She doesn't have to be here again." He turns to her, now that she has finished her crumpets and is sipping some tea.

"Béatrice, is your power off as well? Do you have heat?"

"The heat is on… rawwk! On the street." Jughead starts singing loudly, flapping his wings. Béatrice may not be fluent in English, but she definitely knows this is funny. She starts chuckling and coughing into a napkin.

Jughead picked that one up from me, I must confess. I have a slight obsession with early 80's tunes. Poor boy, stuck back in time. I do prefer his singing to his swearing, though. He hasn't called out angry curse words in a couple days. I think he's happier in this environment, with Tripp and I looking after him, and with Coffee for company, although she tends to think she's the boss of him.

Nineteen

Hannah

I get up quickly, walk over to his cage and feed him a few pieces of papaya and mango. I know he must feel cooped up in there, but there's no way I'm letting him fly around the room. Even when I clean the cage, I don't let him out. I don't want to risk losing him. Not with conditions being what they are outside.

"Jughead is incorrect. I have no heat, but is ok," Beatrice explains. "I have small wood stove. I placed another set of sandbags along shore late last night. Was very cold job, but I got it done…" She smiles at us, and I want to wrap my arms around her and give her a hug. Sandbagging, all alone, in this weather?

"The waters are still rising? No one's come to help? You could lose your home."

"No one knows I'm there, I don't think, no." She looks down at her lap. It's true, if the girl has been trying to avoid the government putting her in foster care, she wouldn't want them discovering her situation.

"But you're eighteen now, right? It's okay. I'm going to call some people." Tripp gets up and heads to the kitchen, and then I hear him sighing. "That is, if my phone isn't dead, I can call some people."

"I have a portable power bank," I call to him. "That should help." I haven't used the power bank on my own phone yet and suddenly realize Mom may be worrying about me. I haven't texted her since I arrived here. Come to think of it, I haven't even checked to see if Good Nights has responded to my complaint. And yet, it doesn't matter anymore. This is surreal. A couple days ago I was miserable about having to share my space with Tripp. Now, I don't want to leave.

"Of course, you brought a power bank, Princess," he calls back playfully. "Uh," I hear him add a second later, "can I take back the teasing? I think I'm going to need that."

"You bet," I call back, smiling to myself. Two days ago, who on earth would have thought he'd actually ask me for my help?

"I must go clean now." Beatrice starts to get up.

"What? You're kidding, right? We have to save your home! This one is solid and on a hill. We don't mind a few dust bunnies. I'll clean it later if I have to. Let's go sandbag."

"You?" She looks at me, glances down at my knee, then looks back up into my eyes.

I think I've just offered to clean toilets on my vacation for this young girl. I'm not used to this version of me. I like her, but I'm not used to her.

I give her a smile, then take her by the shoulder, leading her to the kitchen where we can join forces with Tripp. I'm limping this morning, but not as badly as yesterday. The Advil and slow movement seem to be helping. Mom always told me I was a terrible patient, but I can't just lie on the couch all day. I desperately want to help this girl, so I hope Tripp doesn't veto my choice to go with them.

When we reach the kitchen, Tripp is on the phone, probably on its last bit of battery juice. A few seconds later he finishes his call and hands it to me.

"You go plug this one and your own phone into the power pack, and Béa and I will start making some sandwiches with whatever's still cool in the fridge. We're going to work up some hunger out there."

I love how this man moves right into action, and that he's involved me without hesitation. Doug used to exclude me from so many parts of his life. I never felt like we were a team. I nod, and as I slowly turn to go, he takes me by the waist and turns me back to look at him.

"You sure this isn't too much for you? I don't want that knee getting any worse."

"I'm probably not going to be the greatest help to you with moving the sandbags around, but I can at least tie the things and serve up food. Don't worry."

Béatrice has her back to us, already buttering some bread, but it's not the privacy I seek. Suddenly, this rather large house feels crowded. I wish I could grab Tripp by his biceps, nestle my face into that beard, kiss his full lips. I'm going to be dreaming about that the entire time we're working out along the shore.

"Rawk? Can you feel it? Burning, burning, burning." Jughead's singing my favorite 80's tune again. Coffee pokes her head around the kitchen door and barks at him, and he goes quiet. As I walk away, I hear Tripp chuckling, then explaining to Béatrice how Jughead's moved on from angry curse words to cheesy 80's classics.

Once I've butt-scootched my way up the stairs, I plug both phones in the power bank on the oak dresser, then head to my bathroom and take a couple ibuprofen out of my toiletries case. I take them with water, setting aside a few more to put in my jeans' pocket for later, then sit on my bed, pull up my nightshirt, and inspect my knee.

The swelling has gone down a little, but the side of it feels heavy, as though weighed down with a rock inside it, and painful with every movement. I can't let Tripp know. He'll focus on getting me better, maybe even getting me to a hospital on the mainland, when all I really want is to stay here with him and help this sweet girl. I can't stop picturing that anxious look in her dark brown eyes, over and over in my mind; and now that Tripp has told me her story, I can't forget that she's hiding years of fear and loneliness behind that friendly smile.

It's a struggle, but I manage to carefully pull on my jeans and an old white t-shirt that I don't mind getting dirty. I look in the mirror and begin to brush my hair when I hear a familiar yet jarring tone.

Chirrrp. Chirrrp. Chirrrrp.

Facetime call from Jillian! the screen reads. It sounds like a canary that swallowed an old Internet dial up server, or a vibrator, or both. Either way, the canary is growing increasingly agitated.

I haven't thought about networking or connecting to the outside world for nearly two days now. It's weird. When I first got here, all I could think about was tweeting out my problems to strangers, telling everyone what I was doing, and then contacting Good Nights for a refund. Then, our service got disrupted, our lights went out, and Tripp and I connected with one another. I haven't missed the outside world for one second since he carried me over to that dinner table.

I grab my phone, sit on the bed and slide the button to accept the call. Jill's grinning face lights up my screen.

"Hannah Storm. You live and breathe!"

"I do. I'm sorry. I'm fine. We had no power, no cell service. This means it's back! I hope you weren't too worried."

Jill is lying on a crisp white hotel bed, her phone attached to some fancy clip on the bedside table. "I wasn't too bad, since you told me you were seeking adventure, but I didn't expect you to pull a total Huck Finn. Your Mom and a few other people are having mild panic attacks. I can text her right after this if you want, but you should Facetime her next."

"Can you tell her I'm fine? I'll get in touch, but I can't right now."

"It's two a.m. here in L.A., same in Burnaby. Maybe wait a little." She chuckles. "I have to be on set early today, then we're breaking for a bit. Why are you up before noon on vacation?"

"I'm heading out to help make and stack sandbags."

"Stack sand what?" Jill raises one eyebrow. "I'm going to start calling you Huck! What kind of writer's retreat actually puts you to work outdoors? I thought you writers just sat around, waxing poetic and sipping wine."

"Nice, real nice." I chuckle, shaking my head at her with a disapproving look. "There's a bad flood here, but Tripp Wilson, the guy I'm living with, is awesome at outdoorsy stuff, so he's going to show me how to save someone's home on the shore using sandbags."

"The guy you're living with? And he's a hero, too? How much can one BFF miss in just three days? I had to check my weather app for your area to get a clue." Jill looks amused, but perplexed.

"I texted you and my mom about him—who he is, how he's building an aviary here on the island, didn't you two get it? Good Nights flubbed up, in a major way, booking us both for the same dates. But it's turned out… more than okay…" I smile at her.

"Oh my God. You're thumping thighs with him!"

"Stop it!" I giggle. "Not yet." I smirk.

"Well, when the bedroom rodeo begins, be sure to saddle up!" She's snort-laughing now.

"Jill. It's not like that. He's different. It's different."

Jill looks at me and bites her lower lip.

"Oh, wow. So this is serious? I didn't think… after Doug… wow. I'm so happy for you."

"Well, I'm not sure he's ready, and I'm not sure I want to be the first one after… after he lost his wife in the London bombing."

Jill is shocked into silence for half a second. "Woah. Yea, that's rough. Fine line. He'll let you know. Just have fun for now! So, I guess you're staying…"

"I really want to. Plus, the bridge is out, so I'm kind of stuck here…"

"About that." I can't read her expression now. It's weird, an unfamiliar look on someone so familiar to me. "Uh… Doug got a little worried when I mentioned to him that you were in the flooded area of France. He might be, um, like… looking into rescuing you or something?"

"What the… why were you even talking to him? Why?" I sit up straighter, my shoulders tense. I can feel my cheeks flushing red with anger.

"I'm sorry, sweetie, he's here in LA. He's a producer on our show now! I've seen him every day for the last week. He asks about you. I think he misses you."

"Well, he should have thought about that when he was bonking the brunette."

She looks down at her lap, unable to look me in the eyes. "I really do think he regrets that. Maybe you should give him another chance. I mean, ten whole years together. And the public misses you. Did you know there's a hashtag, to get you back together?"

"Because hashtags are more powerful than free will, right?" I snicker. Now I really don't miss the outside world.

Twenty

Hannah

"It's hashtag Douannah. It was trending a few days ago. People are tweeting about where you've gone physically and in film. They want you back. They want the two of you back! Maybe you should give him another chance."

"Hashtag Douannah? Another chance? Jill, are you doing drugs? What the hell!" I can't believe she's talking like this. She always hated him! She said he was a phony. What's going on? I want to take this phone and smash it in pieces against the old oak headboard.

"He's an excellent producer, and people make mistakes. You could have your entire life back again—your career, your connections, a billion-dollar home, if you just opened up your mind…"

"I don't want that life back!" I stand up and start pacing the room. "Damnit, Jillian. He got to you. I don't know how, but somehow, he got to you. Hollywood got to you." I hate hearing these words coming out of my mouth, because they're directed at my best friend, but I can't help but feel that they're true.

She sighs and rolls onto her back. "He hasn't gotten to me. He made me the head writer on this project, Hani! He's really so very brilliant. Have you forgotten that? I think maybe if you just met with him, well, he says you two could co-produce this show. Just think about it. Maybe not to get back with him, but at least so you can work in TV again? Don't you want that?"

I exhale, trying to gather my thoughts. "I don't know exactly what I want right now, but I do know what I don't want. I don't want him. You tell him I don't need rescuing!"

Her image starts flickering, and then her face freezes on the screen, stuck in an expression halfway between confusion and regret.

"Jill? Can you hear me? Did you hear that?" Nothing. There's no sound, and now the screen has gone black. We lost the call. Crap!

"Power's back. Everything okay?" Tripp's standing in the doorframe, a quizzical expression on his face. I'd mistakenly left the door open.

"Yeah, I noticed that. I'm fine, thanks." I turn away, trying not to look ruffled. "I'll leave this phone here, and we can take yours. It's at eighty percent already." I turn off my phone and leave it on the dresser. I do not want any more calls from Jill! Then, I unplug Tripp's phone from the powerpack and turn back around. Maybe if I look at his face and get lost in those eyes, I'll calm down a little.

"Great. I'll make those calls now. Gather the troops."

"How do you know who to contact?" I ask.

"Spidey senses." He smiles and drifts over to me. He hands me the godawful "slicker" and then, as if on second thought, takes my hand and places it in the left arm of the jacket. He helps me put it on, then slips the blue hood over my head and gently pulls my hair out, raking it with his fingers. Our lips are inches apart. I'm dying here. Dying. He could do this all day. Stroke my hair, stare into my eyes. I would never complain.

"Can I do this?" he asks quietly, his lips moving closer to mine. I lift my chin and close my eyes, anticipating a heavenly moment.

"All done!" Béatrice appears at the door with a wicker basket, and we break apart. "I find so cute picnic basket. We make work, fun time!" She grins at us while Tripp runs his fingers through his hair, sighs, and backs away from me.

Arghh! I moan inside my mind. We were so close! I'll have to be satisfied with hot daydreams, for now, while I shovel sand along the flooded shores, wearing a slicker that makes me look like a big blueberry.

"Aussi, un autre chose," Béatrice smiles.

Her optimism is infectious; I can't but help smile back at my new friend as we make our way downstairs.

"My friends, the ones I had in Côte d'Ivoire? They call me Béa. You save my house—you save me. You call me Béa."

Twenty-one

Tripp

Béa lives in a tiny white cottage with dark green shutters, twenty minutes west of our rental home. It's about five large-man-sized steps from the shore; I know this because for the last half hour, I've been carrying heavy sandbags from the mound of sand that was her garden by her door, across the lawn, over to the water's edge.

The rising waves have already worn down so much of Béa's shoreline, I'm afraid the war is already over, but I can't tell the women this. Not yet. I have to at least give this a fighting try.

"'Idyllic island off the south of France,' my rain-soaked ass! I'm going to have a strongly worded conversation with Value-Added Vacations about this when I get back. Gormless gannets." I groan as I toss another sandbag onto the small pile that's starting to collect beside what was once Béa's garden.

Hannah throws her head back, laughing loudly as she ties a green tag around the top of a sandbag, securing it with her long, perfectly manicured fingers. The sound of her laughter echoing along the shore is more striking than any bird song I've heard in my entire life. It feels like musical medicine for my aching back.

"Value-Added Vacations, nice one. Did you ever think of this as a holiday? I thought your birding was a serious science. The kind of work where spoiled screenwriters weren't welcome." She winks.

"I'm kidding, of course," I say, digging my shovel further into the pile of sand that's been created beside Béa's house. I wish she hadn't dug up her pretty little tulip garden last night. If I'd only known about her troubles, I'd have had my construction buddies deliver some sand earlier. "I have a confession about that."

"Oh, no… what is it this time? Bloody hell, you're not British." She feigns shock.

I chuckle. "Well, I'm thirsty for a Guinness and salivating for mushy peas right now, what do you think?"

"I think that sounds completely gross but authentic." She drags another sandbag over to the heap and leaves it there for me to lift, purposefully hiding the pain she must be feeling in her knee. I never would have called her a 'trooper' the first day I met her. Now, she's rightfully earned that name.

"So, what's the confession?" She blows on her cold fingers, rubs them together, then tucks them deep inside the pockets of her blue slicker.

I stop working for a second, leaning half my weight on my shovel, and look at her. "When we first met, I didn't want to have to explain to you how I started taking time off because of my mental health… I wasn't sure how you'd take it. Now I can tell you—I'm on sabbatical from the museum. They say I can come back to work whenever I'm ready." I exhale, and for a moment, I forget where we are. "Honestly, I've never felt more ready than I have with you, these last few days."

"I make you want to leave and go back to work? Gosh, I'm more high-maintenance than I thought!" She chuckles.

"No, Numpty Gal, you make me feel healthy."

"Oh." I can see her neck is a little mottled, and now her face is flushing pink. "I think you just inserted an insult into a compliment, but I'll let it slide this time, since you're currently breaking your back trying to save our friend's home."

I lift her sandbag onto the pile and start to stack them in a pyramid shape. God willing, more muscles will be here to help me soon. I'm fit, but I'm no Thor.

Twenty-two

Tripp

"There's more. I was given three-hundred and fifty thousand pounds this year, because of Maggie's death." I look down at the overturned earth at my feet as I try to get the rest of my words out.

"I was part of a class action suit that wore me down, physically and emotionally, by the time it was finally over. First, I lost Maggie, then I lost a piece of my pride in that bloody pointless lawsuit. I regret ever signing on. As well, all of the families of the victims were given a share of the money raised by charities like the Red Cross."

"Oh…"

"It's a lot of money, but it doesn't bring her back."

"It certainly doesn't. I'm sorry." She swallows hard. I can see that she's blinking back tears.

"I don't want the money. I need to move on. I'm using it all up, spending it all for good."

She looks up at me. "It's so generous, gosh, what you're doing, Tripp. I don't know where this island's mayor has disappeared to…"

"Probably on holiday in the bloody Caribbean. Definitely not answering my calls. The government is too busy dealing with saving all the tourist areas along the shores of France. Those muppets aren't concerned about the aging homes on this island."

"That's shameful. If you hadn't called that construction company, Béa and the others along this shore would have certainly lost their homes. Now they have a shot, at least."

"Helping Béa today, that's just the beginning of my work on this island. I finally feel ready to go back, but I don't want to return to work at the museum. I want to find the Skinks Babbler, to prove it's still alive, and then build the special rare breeds exhibit I was telling you about—an interactive aviary here on the island, for the locals and some tourists."

"Tripp! What an incredible idea. I love it."

"I'm funding the research and the aviary on my own. I don't want to keep working on it alone, though. Not just because there's a colossal mess to clean up in the forest now." I take a deep breath before continuing, "But also because of you." I look her in the eyes and hope she understands what I'm asking her. I don't want her leaving in a month; I don't want her leaving the island at all. I need her here. We all do. Me, Coffee, Jughead, and Béa. All the puzzle pieces finally fit.

"Wait. I thought they sent you here on a grant, you and Evan…"

"Evan was actually just on holiday. He doesn't know I'm on mental health leave—I've told no one but you. He simply wanted to bring his wife Sarah to the island and give me a hand until the weather decided not to cooperate. The museum knows I'm here trying to find the Skinks, but they don't outright support it, because they think it's a lost cause. I don't."

"Even with all that's happened; even with all the delays? It's a little like believing in miracles." She tucks a loose strand of hair behind her ear and comes a little closer.

"Some things just take time. Yes, I do believe in miracles." I drop my shovel and put my arms around her waist, pulling her close to my chest. "Say it with me three times," I whisper in her ear. "I believe in the Skinks…" I laugh at myself and pull away from her ear, looking her straight-on. "I'm sorry. I can be such a naff."

"Don't apologize. I just need to know—do I click my heels as I say it?" She laughs, her body warm and relaxed against mine. "I believe in the Skinks, and I believe in you, Tripp." Her voice softens to a seductive song. "I believe in you. And I'd love to…"

"Hot tea! I have hot tea, Mr. Tripp, Miss Hannah!" Béa is standing on her rickety front steps holding up a wooden tray. Coffee, who we all decided should stay safely away from the shore's edge, gives us a gleeful bark from behind the screen door.

Blimey O'Reilly! I really like Béa and want to help her, but her timing leaves a whole lot to be desired, especially when I've got a whole lot of desire left to be discovered.

Sigh. All of that will have to wait, once again. We have a house to save from flood waters, and then we have to make sure Béa has adequate heat and light.

Hannah lets go of my hand to take a cup of piping hot tea from Béa's tray. "Thanks sweetie," she says, then hands me the other cup. "You got Tripp's camping kettle working okay, then?"

"Was easy. I love to cook like that always," she says. "Simpler better, yes?"

"It is, Béa, yes. Sometimes simpler is better." Hannah nods, blows on and slowly sips her tea, then looks at me. Her expression tells me that she, too, wanted to stay locked in our embrace.

Everything feels like it's changing. Part of me wants to freeze this moment, this simple, ridiculously ordinary, rain-soaked moment, because in this second, I've realized I can't carry on my future plans without Hannah.

When I lost Maggie, I felt that the only way I was going to survive the rest of my life was to just stumble through the motions required of me; make my broken way from one major event to another. Get through her funeral. Get the therapy completed. Get promoted. Go on sabbatical. Find the Skinks Babbler. Build my aviary.

Then, I met Hannah, and I learned that life and love can't be scheduled. Perhaps social media has fooled us into thinking that life's about rushing from one major event to the next, as quickly and as successfully as possible, with thousands of picture-perfect moments to post for every accomplishment. But these last few days of sipping tea, feeding a spoiled bird, walking with my dog and new friend in the woods, and sharing spontaneous dinners in the dark have taught me otherwise. It turns out that the moments between the events are as important as the events themselves.

I'm about to ask Hannah outright if she'll stay with me for the summer, when we hear a loud honking behind us. We quickly turn to find a large back hoe moving across the lawn, seemingly at full throttle. To my relief, it stops just in front of us and our mound of sandbags, and two burly men I recognize as my new friends and future work partners jump out of the cab, waving as they march forward to greet us.

I am of two minds at the moment. One mind wants to help as many people as I can on this spectacular island. The other, and I'm quite sure, in actual fact, that we're not talking about my mind—it wishes the whole world would sod off and leave us alone.

Twenty-three

Hannah

It's nearly dark by the time we pull up into the driveway, but the rain has stopped completely. The sun began setting as we pulled away from the little white cottage, and as we drove in silence, a storm circled over the shore behind us. We saw bits of far-away lightning whenever we looked in the rear-view mirror.

As we get out of the truck, we look over at the eastern sky. Tripp assures me that this storm is closer to the mainland and heading east. The distant lightning is forming streaks of pink and orange-hued light across the sky. These flashes go on and off behind a thin veil of dark clouds.

"It's our own little light show." Tripp smiles as we watch the last of it from the front walkway. "I got us the best seats in the house."

"This is it, then, eh? Sunny and drying up tomorrow?" If it's finally nice, I'm going to want to spend time outside, maybe try a short walk now that the knee is on the mend. Béa and Tripp have unknowingly inspired me to get started on a writing project. Even though I'm nervous to try something new and different, it feels like the perfect fit for my life right now. I can't believe I want to venture into documentary writing, but I think this is what I'm supposed to do next. It's the type of writing that could actually make a difference. Once I get the chance to tell Tripp, I know he'll love the idea, too.

"Only God knows." He exhales, shaking his head. "I'm waiting on the text that tells me to go build an ark."

"But you never have your phone on you, or it's off. You'd miss the message," I tease, starting up the stairs as Coffee contentedly trots along behind me.

"Hey, Numpty Gal, enough, it's on now." He pulls his phone from his back pocket, holds it up, and follows me. "I don't want to miss anything from Béa."

I wait for him under the one lamp lighting the front door, crossing my arms over my chest. "You'd better watch yourself with this new nickname you've got for me, or you'll be called a Grumpet in front of everyone. Marcel and JF included."

"Grumpet?"

"You've got your grumpy moments, and you love to bring me crumpets."

"Ha! The lads would love you for it. They admire a lady who swings her balls in their midst. They couldn't get enough of you, today, and all the tea and sandwiches you brought us."

"I was swinging my balls? Didn't know I had any." I can't stop chuckling. "I wish Béa had taken us up on our offer to stay with us here."

"She's a feisty, independent girl. There was no changing her mind," he says. "I'm relieved we managed to hold back the water and keep her safe."

"Marcel and JF are so strong and perfect gentlemen, too. I think they'll be a real asset to your aviary project."

"Give them a few pints and they have their moments, though." He shakes his head. "We had a few rounds over at JF's place, a celebration of sorts, two nights before you arrived."

"Moments? I doubt their language compares. You don't want to hear the kind of comments that come out of some construction worker's mouths in downtown L.A."

"Oh, I can imagine." He puts his left hand at my lower back and ushers me inside. The contact between us is electric. It's a powerful charge moving up my spine—fuel for my neck, lips, breasts. I don't know why here, why now, standing at the front door, waiting to get inside, but I cannot stop thinking about taking off my clothes and how I can get Tripp involved in that task.

We both fall silent, kicking off our wellies, shaking out our wet hair. He puts his phone on the foyer table and takes off my slicker for me, hanging it on the brass hook by the door. Then, silence. We're just standing here, staring at each other, and I forget to breathe. Finally, Coffee breaks the silence, and I remember to exhale.

"Woof!" This noise, in turn, wakens Jughead.

"Wazzup, peeps, wazzup?"

Tripp laughs. "Is that one your fault as well, Hannah?" he asks. It is something I said back home a lot, but I don't answer. I'm crouched down, busy feeding Coffee dog biscuits from the jar in the oak cabinet.

"Well, at least he hasn't called me a wankpuffin yet!"

"Tripp! Now he's going to say exactly that!" I stand and shake my head.

"You're moving better," he says.

"Thanks to your doctoring, it's definitely on the mend," I say.

"Excellent. I just realized something." Tripp walks over to Jughead's cage and feeds him the special cracker pieces we've set aside in containers. "The power's back on, but the lights are still all out in here!"

"Leave them off." I blurt it out, feeling bold.

Our eyes lock. He sends me a smoldering look from across the room, and then, before I know what's happened, he's right in front of me, his arms engulfing me, his lips on mine.

His kiss is strong, full of passion and desire. The warmth and surprise sensation of his lips finally touching mine makes me lose my balance a little, and my left knee buckles. He feels this and stops kissing me, but his hands keep caressing both sides of my face.

"Are you feeling alright? Do you want me to stop?" He brushes a damp strand of hair off my eyes as he looks into them.

"No, I mean, yes, I'm perfectly fine, and no," I catch my breath, "don't ever stop."

The second he hears this, Tripp reaches down, swiftly picks me up and begins to carry me up our wooden stairs. Our stairs. Funny. I keep thinking that.

"Tripp," I whisper, "watch your step, it's so dark." The darkness is heightening my emotions and desire and his, I'm sure, but I can barely see what's in front of me. I decide to just trust in him and bury my face into that crook between his neck and shoulder, giving him little kisses along his neck and Adam's apple as he pushes my bedroom door open with his foot.

I was secretly hoping he'd bring us to this room, because it has the gorgeous, massive four-poster bed in it. At this point, however, having wanted him since the moment I set eyes on him, I'd have happily made love to him on a mound of sandbags in the rain.

Tripp places me down on the bed and gives me a "one sec" sign as he fumbles around in the dark. I hear the sound of one match striking a matchbook, then see him lighting the kerosene lamp to my right and feel him crawl over my feet to get to the other side of the bed. He lights the other lamp, then blows out the match. A sexy, smoky scent penetrates the air.

"You and your kerosene lamps." I giggle. All of a sudden, I'm nervous. It's been a while. I pull back the bed covers but stay on my back. He crawls over to me, placing his arms to either side of my shoulders, his knees astride my hips, and begins kissing me all over. My forehead, my eyelids, my cheeks, my lips, my neck, then my lips all over again. Over and over. I melt into his kisses and savor every bit of electricity building inside me, feeling more relaxed with each new sensation.

"I never thought I'd be able to let love in again, but then you came along," he says, his forearms firm with exertion. "I love you, Hannah."

"I love you too," I whisper, and I know nothing else needs to be said. No talk of my fears or his loss or our future. It's just us, here and now, our bodies coming together as one.

I sit up, and he follows my lead, sitting back on his ankles. I lean in and kiss his mouth, nibbling his lower lip as I start to pull off his t-shirt. He raises his arms to help me, and my eyes take in the muscular masterpiece that is his chest and abs. Now I don't have to just look to admire them. I glide my hands over his pec muscles and shoulders, back and forth and around, then bring my mouth to one nipple and lick it carefully, flicking my tongue in a circular motion.

Tripp moans, his head back, eyes closed. Encouraged by this, I make my way to the other nipple, sucking it slowly, methodically, until his groans grow increasingly loud and impassioned.

"C'mere, Sweetness," he says, lifting my face up to his. He takes my mouth and covers it with his, his tongue flicking and probing mine. His hands tug at the bottom of my shirt, so I raise my arms until the shirt is over my head, off and away, tossed to the floor. I reach for the button on his jeans, release it and watch as he wiggles out of them and his boxers, tossing them to the floor. My jeans and thong quickly join the bundle of clothes. His eyes catch mine in the wavering light, and I see them crinkling up at the corners with amusement and anticipation.

We're facing one another, naked on our knees, and I can't help but think: far from strangers anymore. He puts his hands on my waist, pulling my body tightly to his.

"So bloody tired of sharing my space with you," he says with an animalistic growl, no trace of a smile. "I want you out first thing in the morning."

I start to pull away, but his eyes laugh as they meet mine in the lamplight, giving him away. He strokes my hair, kisses my breasts.

"That's fine, no biggie," I play along, "I just hope Good Nights lives up to its name tonight."

"Oh, Sweetness," he growls. He's so irresistible like this. He pushes me down onto the bed, lowering his arms just a little, our lips inches apart. "You'll be walking funny tomorrow but begging for a sixth star."

I start to laugh, but he covers my mouth with his, his eyes full of desire and intent. He lowers his body to mine slowly, his warm chest touching my breasts, then backs off. What a tease! He lowers and kisses me, then pulls away slightly, lowers and kisses again until I can't take anymore, and I'm wrapping my legs around him, pulling him closer, begging him for more with my eyes, my pelvis, my entire body.

When he's deep inside me and we're rocking together as one, I moan out loud, clawing his back with my nails. He's primitive, but he touches me in all the right places. It's fiery, raw, beautiful. This is the best sex I've ever had. How have I been missing out on this feeling my whole life?

The sensations rise like waves at high tide, culminating to a peak, until neither of us can take any more. We surf to the shore together, calling each other's names and several curse words. When we fall to our backs, spent, I feel wetness on my right cheek, but can't tell if the tears are mine or Tripp's. I get my answer when he turns his head to look at me, his eyes moist, a smile across his face.

"You are beyond beautiful," he says, and I drift into deep, blissful sleep.

Twenty-four

Tripp

Hannah is still asleep when my eyes open to the early morning light. I sit up slowly and watch her while she dreams. Her rosebud lips are pursed like a small, innocent newborn; her long eyelashes flutter like a butterfly's wings in the breeze. She's my Snow White, pale and pristine, asleep in a field of flowers.

OHoogahhhh!

OHooogahhhhhh!

Blimey! She snores. And loudly!

So, maybe not like a butterfly, or a princess. Definitely not silent.

I pull on my boxers and jeans, which I find on the floor among our pile of tossed clothes, then stand and listen to her for another moment, trying to recall what other noises I've come across in my life that are akin to this alarming new Hannah sound. I finally get it as I start down the stairs. She sounds like two teenagers with air horns, competing for attention at a football game. And the sound my first car made when it stalled at stop signs.

'Hello, Master Luke." Jughead squawks when he sees me, and then he chortles. I wouldn't think he has any clue what the bloody names he's calling us mean, except there's that drawn-out guffaw he always makes at the end! We may have a maniacal dictator here, disguised in a macaw costume.

"No Jughead," I say in a low whisper, with hopes that he didn't already wake Hannah. "Don't you know by now? My name is Tripp."

"Get a grip, Tripp." There's that guffaw again.

"I don't mind if I don't. I'm perfectly content sitting on cloud nine right now." I feed him a cracker, and then I start whistling an old tune Dad taught me. I'm not sure why it came to mind now, but I'm moved with the memory of sitting on Dad's lap in his office, back when he was content. "There'll be mango soon, buddy, hang in there. Gotta go make eggs for my gal."

"You're our only hope."

I shake my head but can't shake my smile. He's somehow morphed from a cursing child macaw into a movie-obsessed tween. We need to get him a girlfriend—keep him occupied and out of trouble.

I head to the kitchen, noticing how bright and sunny it is in each room. The dining area looks completely different, and I can't help but think about serving Hannah breakfast here soon. I feel a spring in my steps; what a beautiful day to be alive. I spread a little oil around the frying pan on the stove, then open the fridge to find that it's nearly empty. Thankfully, two eggs remain, and I think there are about a half dozen of my crumpets left. I could show Hannah how to make them. We'll have to grab a few supplies at the corner store this afternoon.

"Hi, you."

Hannah strolls into the kitchen wearing just a white t-shirt and panties, her long legs and slender bum seducing me with every step. Her puffy eyes and tousled hair remind me of every single move we made under those sheets last night. I've heard of bad hair days, but I think this is what women call "a disaster." Tousled at the top, sticking out like she jammed her fingers in a socket before coming down for tea. I want to wrap it and her around me and take her back to bed.

"Sweetness. Good morning." I kiss her softly and hand her a cup of piping hot tea.

"You're spoiling me. It's going to be a hard decision." She leans back against the kitchen counter and blows on her tea. I notice her breasts are like perfectly round tennis balls, her nipples hard in that t-shirt she's wearing. Wait, isn't that my t-shirt?

"Decision?" I can't quite concentrate on what she is saying, now that I realize she's wearing a white lace thong under my shirt.

"Yea," she sighs. "I checked my phone just now. The bridge has reopened and flights are open too."

I flip the eggs with a spatula, put them on simmer, change my crestfallen expression to one she won't be able to read, and turn around.

"You're leaving?"

"I don't want to, Tripp." She looks sad, but also a little panicked. "I just… I don't know… how long can we play house? Really? I need to get back to reality, find a new job, try to sell my old place."

"This is reality, Sweetness. Just because it's doing us both some good doesn't mean it's not real."

Hannah sips her tea, puts it down, and wraps her arms around me. I'm relieved for the physical contact from her, but utterly confused why she's pulling away emotionally.

"I know, but, I used to have my own television show, and now, I'm nothing."

"You aren't nothing to me. You're everything." I pull her in close and kiss her tenderly.

"Oh, Tripp," she says, pulling away. "I love you. I do. But we're living in a bubble here on this island. It's just not practical. Maybe I can come back on the Good Nights refund when I land a new TV show, and things are sorted back home. The app's date and time are still frozen to the day and hour I arrived here, but they sent me a form letter in the direct messages, and I received it. I guess they sent it to all of their customers. We're getting a full refund and our next stay is free."

I feel like a knife has gone straight through my heart. Twice. "What's so wrong with a bubble? We've been far from slacking. We've been doing some good for others, and we can keep doing that together. We've done more in a few days than some people do all of their lives."

"I agree. I know. It's just, Jill told me there may be this LA gig… she said I have a chance to revive my career… she's my best friend. I'm torn…"

"L.A.?" I pull back and look into her eyes. "You had a wild and wonderful idea to make a documentary. It's as anti-L.A. as it goes. Be brave, Han. Make the thing. Spend the summer with me. I spoke with the owner this morning. He says he isn't planning on coming back…"

"The whole summer…" She sighs as her lips curl up into a slight smile. Maybe I'm finally getting somewhere.

"Yes, can you imagine?" I give her a gentle squeeze. "Last night, we said we loved each other. Can't we explore 'us' a while longer?"

"I still can't believe how fast this has happened to us. I mean, I feel it too… but… how?"

"How?"

"How did this happen?"

"I don't bloody know! You stormed into my life, true to your name, with an angry bird in your hand. How could I not take notice of you?" Hannah's eyes grow wide, and her expression changes. I see love.

"Let's put aside the fact that I'm an ornithologist and that seemed a bit like divine intervention. Or the fact that you're clever, independent, and you want to help all creatures, even petulant birds, grumpy Brit buggers, and teenagers who speak another language. You're also the most beautiful woman I've ever seen in my life. How could I not fall in love with you?

I can feel Hannah's knees buckle under her, so I tighten my grip and turn her so her back is against the counter.

"What if this doesn't work out?" she asks, her voice quivering. She exhales deeply before saying anything more. "I mean, I have to go back to Canada, and you live in forking Oxford. I've never been, don't even know what it looks like, and you're going to go back home too, and probably break my heart. Or what if it's me who disappoints you? I know you never thought you'd find love again. What if I'm not what you want?"

That's enough. Enough overthinking for one morning. I swiftly grab her around her waist and lift her onto the counter.

"What if you stop throwing a wobbly, and I kiss all those worries away?"

For the first time this morning, I hear her melodic laugh, and it calms me.

"Counter sex is so underrated," I say. "The granite stuff, that's cold, but the older models; this smooth, thick maple butcher block that we've got going here? Yea baby, that's the stuff wet dreams are made of."

"Uh," she smirks at me, "so then, you've been experiencing counter sex alone?" I notice we're nearly eye-level now.

"No, Numpty Gal!" I chuckle. "No, I was being poetic. You're the writer—thought you'd like that."

"Would you just shut up and do me?"

"I would be happy to oblige." I grab hold of the counter with one hand and stroke her lovely bare thighs with the other as our lips come together.

Our kisses are even more powerful than last night. So powerful, I'm afraid I'll lose my balance, and she'll come tumbling down with me. I hold on to her tighter, but I'm not worried about a few bruises in the name of love.

If this is our last day together, we need to make some memories to take home with us.

Twenty-five

Tripp

There are white, foamy bath bubbles everywhere. In her hair, on our arms and legs, overflowing onto the floor. It's a beautiful mess.

After we exhausted the kitchen counter, I carried Hannah upstairs to the roomy four-poster bed. I didn't once check a clock, but I knew when our morning of lovemaking had turned to early afternoon. I could tell by the soft, soulful light flowing down and around Hannah's ginger hair and pale skin. It shone through the white sheers in such a hallowed way, it reminded me of sunlight coming through a cathedral's stained-glass windows. I sighed with deep contentment as I curled into her body. If these holy hours with Hannah were akin to attending church, well, then I'd just made up for missing a decade's worth of confessional.

"A penny for your thoughts?" I smile at Hannah's choice of expression and sink further down under the bubbly froth, my head resting comfortably between her breasts. She has been spending too much time with this Brit, and it's rubbing off on her language, but too much time is never enough. I slowly rub her calves with my soapy hands, then pull her legs gently up and around my knees. She's wrapped around me like a big red Christmas bow. My toes just touch the edge of the soaker tub, and it's deep enough to cover the both of us with suds and water. I don't want to leave. I will shrivel up in this hot water, but I shall die a happy man.

"I was thinking how I've never taken a bubble bath before, and that I could quite get used to this."

"You've never taken a bath?" I can't see her face, but she sounds incredulous.

"I've taken baths, my mum made me do so, of course, but not long, lingering bubble baths, and never one with another person."

"Another first for us, then. We need to call Guinness World Records and record these achievements." She chuckles.

"I'm not calling anyone, all day, and possibly not a soul on this Earth ever again." I take her hand and start to give it a gentle massage with my thumb. I read that hand massages are important for people who type a lot. "Bea is working, and the flood waters have receded, but we can check in on her tomorrow. We have this afternoon and evening all to ourselves."

"Oh, that's wonderful. This hand thing you're doing and our alone time."

"You like that?"

"Yea, I love it. So sensual. No one's ever done it for me before."

"Has anyone given you a nickname?" I rub her knuckles.

"Besides Hani, which I hate? Not really. I liked it when you called me Sweetness."

I feel myself blush, recalling the heat of our bodies coming together for the first time last night. Combined with the steam lifting off the water, I'm feeling somewhat light-headed. "I wasn't thinking much when I came up with that, if you recall…"

"So then, it was organic. Unforced. I like that. I think you need a pet name."

"Oh no! No bloody pet name for me!"

"Well, I can take Numpty Gal... even though I know it's an insult."

"It is, and it isn't," I say, stroking her forearm. "I tend to show affection to those I love through insults. It's my heritage."

"Oh yes, that cold British heart. Showing affection with insults. My gramps did that. He called me Dum-Dum."

"Dum-Dum?" I laugh.

"Yes, and I loved it. He even wrote me a poem in my autograph book when I was five:

" 'When I sit down,

"I often get numb bum,

"and when I get numb bum,

"I think of my Dum-Dum!' "

"Oh, that is clever. Your gramps was funny."

"And Granny was a darling with an infectious chuckle. I miss them." She sighs, and I feel her back sinking further down into the water. I sink along with her.

"Well then, in their honor, Numpty Gal it is," I say. "You know, the first day we met, I called you Princess in my mind, but you're much more than that. You've led a spoiled life, yes, but you recognize it, and you give back. You're a treat. In fact," I begin kissing her fingers, overdoing it for the comedy. "You're so delicious… I should call you sweet cakes."

"Ew!" She sits up a little and throws me off balance.

"Crumpet?" I try again. She's laughing now, and it's making my whole chest shake under the suds.

"Fairy cake?" I'm kidding, and she knows it.

"Um, no. No thanks. Sweetness. That's good. But I'm definitely calling you Grumpet."

"Yea, yea… no nicknames for me."

"Oh, so it doesn't go both ways?

"Both ways? Oh, we could do it all the ways, if you want."

She starts throwing suds at me, narrowly missing my eyes. I slowly turn around on my knees and retaliate, splashing some water on her, along with the suds.

"Stop!" she says amid a fit of giggles. "We're making a mess!" Despite her pleas for me to stop, she keeps splashing me until I grab her hands and kiss her, hard. Our bubble fight is soon forgotten.

We're wrapped in the cozy white waffle robes James left hanging in the en-suite bathroom, sitting in the sunshine of the bedroom balcony, listening to the chirping field crickets and softly cooing stock doves. I feel like we're on a cruise ship in a roomy first-class cabin. We can see the deep blue edges of the ocean just beyond the coniferous trees out front. After days of high winds and rain, I could do without the rocking of the ship, so this view on solid ground, from the balcony, is perfect. We've made spicy Chai tea and toast to add to this feast for our five senses.

"Will you stay the summer?" I blurt it out, seeing no reason to pretend this isn't important to me.

Hannah looks at me. "I don't know Tripp. I don't know. I mean, I got this idea to write a documentary about this island, to try to force the French government to revitalize the homes along the shore, so they can use them for tourism. That way, the visitors to your Aviary would have a low-budget place to stay."

She's brilliant. "Tourism can spoil an island, but if we keep it under careful watch, it could help the people living here, yes. I've already hired an environmentalist for my project, to keep it all in check. I hadn't thought about where all the visitors would stay."

"Not everyone can afford a mansion on a hill." She smiles and points out two ferryboats crossing each other's paths. They're back in working order.

"True. The cottages would be perfect. They'd keep people from simply camping in the forest, although, I'm trying to set up restrictions anyway." I haven't had time to tell her yet how I need Oxford's help to assure our special forest becomes a protected area. It's going to take years, but I'll build the open Aviary on the edge, where we parked our car, and apply for environmental protection for the rest of the forest. If I find the Skinks, that will certainly help move the process along.

"Maybe there's a way you could be involved in fixing the cottages up, too. I loved what you did for Béa."

"The sweeping? The flowers in the vase? I don't know, I may have picked her goldenrod! I'm not up to speed on my French wildflowers." She's blowing on her tea again. I can't get enough of that.

"They looked beautiful. You're beautiful. I'll help you out with the documentary. Please, stay with me here."

She looks at me for a second, then exhales, grinning. "Okay, I'll do it. Let's do it. I'll write the documentary, but I need to go back in a couple weeks to get my old house sold and grab a few more clothes and…"

I pull an imaginary, futuristic visor from off the top of my head, down over my eyes. "Clothes? Where we're going, we don't need clothes."

"Will you stop being a naff!" She laughs, then gets up and sits on my lap, wrapping her arms loosely around my neck. I'm so relieved that she's staying. As we watch the ferry boats coast along the restless sea, I quietly thank the angels who sent her here to me.

Twenty-six

Tripp

"Do you trust me?" I say, as I balance the teal blue bicycle on the gravel road for her one more time, hoping she'll climb on.

"Oh, I trust you. It's that beast of a bicycle I don't trust," she says, and she takes a step back. So much for getting somewhere. Or getting groceries.

I carefully lean the bicycle against the side of the garden shed and walk over to her, taking her hand in mine.

"Right. I know this is new for you." I give her hand a squeeze. "But you wanted to try new things and not say no!"

"It's not me. It's my knee. My knee says no." She pouts.

"But it's tandem. I've read all about this. I take the lead, and you're 'stoker.' I do all the work, and your legs just move as I pedal us along. It's physiotherapy. It will be good for you."

"A cup of tea and lots more sex would be better for me." She lets go of my hand and crosses her arms over her chest. I'm about to taunt her with 'Princess Hani,' just to see if that convinces her to take the ride with me when she walks over to the bike and caresses the black leather seat with one hand. Oh, she's thinking about it. Definitely going there.

"Okay," she says, turning to look at me. "In the name of trying new things and physiotherapy, I'll do ten minutes."

"That's great! That's all we need to get us to the store and back."

"I miss room service."

"Hannah…" I tousle her hair. "I'll cook for us when we get back. Sunset dinner."

"I was kidding," she says as I pull the bicycle out and set it in the right direction for us. "I've loved being alone in this house, on this island. No phone calls every five minutes, no assistants telling me what I'm supposed to do next. It's such a radical change from my old life."

"I would think so, hashtag Douannah." I smile at her as she pulls her weaker leg over and straddles the back seat. I make sure that she's steady, checking her hip and feet position.

"How the? How'd you know?" She doesn't look upset, just slightly startled that her old life has intercepted her new one.

"Paper delivery started up again this morning," I say, my hand steady on her hip. "I guess James subscribes. Found it on the woven front doormat. You and your ex are on page thirteen. I didn't realize Doug was so… so big-money. Big-time," I say, realizing how ridiculously jealous I sound.

"He was. He was the lead in a TV sitcom that was very popular a few years ago. After doing Broadway for a while and getting mixed reviews, his star lowered in Hollywood's celestial sky. His publicist has been working overtime lately trying to assure that he—and because it helps him, me—are trending again."

"Trending? It's not Hot or Not anymore?" I wonder if I'll ever understand this world she comes from.

"It's a Twitter thing. Did it say we're a couple again? Because we aren't, if you're worried about that."

"It was mostly about him signing on for a new 'it shall not be named' TV show. All rather cloak and dagger, if you ask me." I bend to check that the bike's tires are properly inflated. "Sells more papers I suppose."

"That world is about that, yes. Selling. Hearts and feelings don't seem to matter."

"Well, the interviewer mentioned the hashtag, and Doug replied something about how 'your love may be forever engraved on the public's heart.'"

"Oh, barf. Can we just go? I don't really want to spend our date talking about my ex." She sighs.

"Me neither," I say, and I climb onto the bike's lead seat. "You ready to be 'stoker'?"

"Not too stoked, no. But I wasn't ready to meet you, either," she chuckles. "Let's do this."

Oh, this woman. One moment she's throwing a wobbly and insisting on the Wi-Fi password, the next, she's an adventure-seeking, forest-hiking, tandem-biking babe. The bloody shocking thing is, I like all of it, because she's being authentic. At least she's never fake with me. I don't know if I'm going to be able to handle all of her moods, but I want to. I want to imitate her when she's grumpy, make her laugh, and hold her hand through all of our adventures.

As I pedal off the downward sloping driveway and turn left towards the corner store, Hannah calls out a hesitant, "uh oh," followed by a gleeful, "woohooo!" and I know I made the right choice in encouraging her to join me.

The wind feels warm against my face as I pedal into it. It's a humid afternoon with a slight taste of sea salt in the air. I'll take that over the cool, unrelenting rain we had a few days ago. The road we're on is nearly treeless, winding its way through shimmering fields of gold.

"You doing okay there?" I call behind me.

"I'm great. This feels good, actually. I'm surprised."

Just as she says it, a family of chickens from a nearby farm appears on the road ahead.

"Put your feet down slowly, I'm going to brake," I say, wobbling a little, but pulling it together just in time. I'm able to slow down, and we pull off to the side and stop to watch the brown mother hen lead her four chicks across the road. As they reach the other side and scurry away into the field I turn back slightly to look at Hannah.

"Now we can say that we witnessed it, and we still don't know."

"Chickens aren't very talkative," she says. "They keep their secrets close to their… chicken breasts…" Now, I'm laughing.

"It's just another minute down the road, but if you're in pain at all, we could walk," I say.

She shakes her head. "I think it's helping stretch everything out. I'm good."

"I'll have to charge you for this exercise, but the massage tonight is free." I smirk.

"Uh huh." She grins. "Just you wait until you get my bill."

The grocer remembers me from last week. "How'd you folks make out in the flooding? Kept dry?"

"Yeah, we're up on the hill, at James Tander's place? Some homes along the shore nearly didn't make it, though." I hand him our small bag of strawberries, peaches, flour, butter, and blueberries.

He wipes his hands on his white apron and arranges several items in my backpack, placing the heavier ones first, just as I asked.

"That would be a shame. Some of those places should be deemed heritage homes." He shakes his head.

I turn to Hannah. "See? We need you." She smiles at me and bites into a peach. "Mmph."

"I could try the lead seat," she says as I adjust my backpack and start to climb on the bike.

"Uh, that's a little too ambitious for today, I think."

"Okay. Tomorrow. After we eat our blueberry crumpets."

As we start our ride home as the sun starts to lower in the sky, I feel something shift behind me, and I have to straighten my handles to readjust our ride. We're fine, and I know what she's doing, just on instinct.

She's got her arms wide open back there, like a little kid running into ocean waves.

"See? I do trust youuuu!" she squeals.

"Get your bloody hands back on the handle bars!" I growl, and after a few seconds more, she obeys. We laugh the whole ride home.

I love her! I love country, bike-riding, peach-kissing Hannah. I wonder if we can simply send for her things in Burnaby. I had to let Mags go without saying goodbye. I don't want to have to utter any goodbyes to Hannah.

Twenty-seven

Hannah

"You know what I like the most about this supper?" I ask, putting my fork down beside my remaining chicken parm and taking a sip of savory red wine.

Tripp has once again gone to extremes to create a romantic setting for us, this time, up on the bedroom balcony. Not only is there a lit kerosene lamp at every corner, but he's also strung up some white lights he grabbed at the corner store. "The grocer said they were Christmas stock. They were dirt cheap," he said when I found him unpacking them. "I figured, we had weird weather in May, why not have a little bit of Christmas as well?"

Once everything was set up on the balcony, we sat in silence and breathed in the perfume below: lily of the valley blooms mingling with wet grass and salty ocean air. The sun is a brilliant orange, fading and lowering below cotton candy clouds. It's pleasant enough for us to be sitting out barefoot and in our waffle robes. They're becoming our go-to 'Let's Stay In' wardrobe, and I cannot believe I have never dressed like this for days at a time before. I've grown fond of my blue slicker, jeans, and this waffle robe. I do not miss constrictive VIP attire one bit.

"What do you like the most? Hm. There's no Entertainment Tonight reporter, asking you how you feel?" he teases.

"Well, there's that. I never had swarms of paparazzi around me. That only happened when I was with Doug."

"Well, then, I say good riddance to all that." He lifts his wine, inhaling its strong oak and vanilla aroma. "Who needs fame and fortune when you can have a quiet balcony dinner with this hot and happening British mug?" He stops and lifts his chin in a GQ-like pose, stroking his beard.

I grin. "Exactly, but there's more." I nibble lightly on my corn. It's dripping butter onto the white ceramic plate on my lap. Why did he have to go and buy messy food for our date?

Tripp sees me hesitating with the corn and smiles politely. He lifts a fork and knife. I think he's going to cut the corn off the cob, but he puts them down again and suddenly dives into his cob with his entire face. I can't see his eyes anymore. He's making noises like Disney's Beast. I have to put my plate down at my feet so it won't fall off my lap, I'm laughing so hard.

"Ahhh, yes that's how it's done in the lowlands, lassie," he says in a Scottish drawl. He lifts his face to look at me. There are pieces of corn all through his beard. Nose. Neck. Even one earlobe. He's absolutely covered in corn.

"You want me badly now, don't ya, baby?" he says with a low growl.

"You are such a Tripp!" I laugh and drift over to him to begin picking the mess out of his beard.

"Oh, so we're monkeys now, is that what we've become?" he asks. "Is that how you see me?"

"We're descended from…"

"Don't. Don't even start. That's not bedtime banter." He pulls me onto his lap, hands on my hips, and starts covering my face in kisses. Corn kisses and a beard burn. I'm glad I'm done eating, because I can't stop laughing.

"Ha! Agreed! Wait!" I say, gasping for air. He holds off with the kisses for a second and starts wiping himself down with a linen napkin. "I was going to tell you what I like most about this balcony meal—no mosquitoes! We would have them up here bothering us by now if we were in Canada, or at least, black flies. I wanted to ask, why is that? But I'm afraid you'll go into one of your long Factoid-man speeches. We should really just enjoy the peace and quiet of this spring evening."

"Well, I'm glad you asked," he begins. "We ornithologists do have to know a lot about entomology, since birds eat bugs, you know."

I roll my eyes. This is going to take a while. Reading my thoughts, as usual, he leans over to the patio table to his left and hands me my wine. "It's spring, and mosquitoes usually aren't a problem here 'til summer, but we're up on a hill, away from the water. They're probably having a party over at Béa's place."

"Oh." I hadn't forgotten about her, but we've been inside a dreamy couple bubble these last twenty-four hours. "Do you think she's okay?"

"She called the house when you were in the bath, actually. She's just fine. Water on her shoreline has receded, and she's warm and happy. I want to visit her tomorrow, though. Tell her we're hiring her for our project."

"We?" I smile at him.

"Slip of the tongue, but, I like how it sounds." He slides one hand under my robe and strokes my lower back.

"Me too." I say. "In fact…" I take a breath, shake off my nerves, and continue. "I kind of like the idea of acting sort of like… adoptive parents to her. Watch out for her. She's eighteen, but she's still young, living alone on this island. She needs somebody. We could be her somebodies."

Tripp looks at me and nods but doesn't say one word. He closes my robe for me, tying it with the belt, then gets up and starts adjusting the white string lights, his back turned. I sit back, dumbstruck. I can't see his expression. What's he thinking? Was that too much?

Oh, I said too much. I went too far, too soon. Damnit! Why can't I do relationships? Why? I'm a savvy negotiator, an Emmy-award winning writer, and a failure at love.

Twenty-eight

Tripp

Parents. She wants us to be parents; like a team.

I'm at a complete loss for words, so I keep my back turned and continue working with the string of lights, pretending that they're tangled. I swallow hard to hold back the tears, so she won't think I'm a wuss. I know she already accepts me for who I am: strengths, weaknesses, goofy man-child. All of it. All of me. That's why I'm so emotional.

I've always wanted to be a dad. To do everything my own dad never did with me. To accept the child for who she is, to help her become her best self. My chance to be a parent with Mags was stolen from me. And then along came Hannah.

I've only known her a short while, but I know her. I know this is our destiny. Hannah and I have a real chance here. A chance to help another human being and ourselves in the process.

So why can't I bloody tell her any of this? Oh my God, I think there's a tear on my cheek. I wipe it away, fast, and turn to take away her plate and mine.

"I should go clean up." I swallow hard again, just in case I look wobbly-chinned. "You just stay here and rest that knee, Sweetness." There. Got out a term of affection. She'll be fine. She'll just think I'm tired. It'll be fine. I did fine.

When I return ten minutes later, Hannah is curled up on the bed with her wine glass in hand, the bed quilt wrapped around her, wearing nothing else. I'm instantly turned on.

"Got a little chilly, but I left the doors open, so we can watch the stars, and our white lights. That is, if you want…" She hands me my half-full wine glass from the bedside table.

"I'd love to," I say. So, we're good, then. I crawl onto the bed slowly and sit back against the pillows she's propped up. I feel my body become less tense as she pulls off my robe, pulls the quilt over me, draws her warm skin close to mine.

"What a view." I say, staring out at the twinkling blanket of stars before us. She's quiet for a moment. That's unusual. I turn to look at her, take her hand, and give it a squeeze.

A second later, she speaks. "When you really look at it, that wide, open sky, it kind of makes everything right in the world again, doesn't it?" she says. "That and walking by the ocean surf roaring in on a clean beach... everything feels bigger than you, and yet a part of you."

"It does," I say, sighing with contentment. I take a long swallow from my glass and set it down again. I know this is exactly when, exactly how I should tell Hannah what I feel. The time is now. Don't waste a minute. Tell her: yes, let's foster Béa. Tell her she's become my whole world, and

I want to grow old with her. I want her and Béa and everything on this island to grow old with us.

I can't. I just can't find the words.

Bugger. I need to call my therapist tomorrow morning, tell him he's total shite, and I want my money back.

We've finished our wine and set down our glasses. I'm gently raking my hands through her ginger tresses, and now that I've turned to her, I manage to tell her how I feel about… Jughead.

"You… love him?" She's looking at me like I've lost it. "Are you quite drunk?"

"It's not the wine. I just mean that, he's grown on me. He's singing bloody eighties' tunes for crying out loud! He's alright with me. When you go away for a couple weeks, to sell the house and all, I'll watch Jughead. He's happy here. In fact, I've grown attached to the bloody petulant parrot."

She shakes her head, smiling. "He is quite special. I told you so when I first got here. But, what about when you're working out in the woods? You can bring Coffee… but Jughead?"

"Well, don't go and spoil it all now. I've made plans for him, okay?"

"You have? Aviary plans? Wow. Can I see them?"

"Let it be a surprise." I say, and she nods silently, to my surprise, letting this one go.

Silence again. What's going on with her? I caress her face. "A penny for your thoughts?"

"I was thinking…" she says softly, closing her eyes. "Of naming this house The Lighthouse."

"Ah, Sorting Hat Hannah. Right. I love The Lighthouse. But why?"

I know it's not shaped like an old lighthouse, but it feels like one. The last few days, it's been lit up only by kerosene lamps…" Her voice sounds sleepy. "Lighthouses really aren't that bright inside, but here, at the top… they're beacons of light for others. We were beacons. Beacons of light, exactly when we needed to be. We drew Béa in. You drew me in…"

"I drew you in, did I…" I can feel my heart pounding in my chest. I think it might explode. I kiss her forehead. Her eyelids. Her lips.

"You drew me in," she whispers, and when I feel her thighs pressing forcefully against mine, I stop thinking altogether. We make love without speaking, sharing an understanding with each other and nature that no one should disrupt the soulful silence of this night. At her peak of passion, she calls my name several times, then bites a pillow to muffle her screams.

That night, my dreams are vivid. I'm running for Maggie in the dark underground, trying to save her. I have no control. She's standing on the platform when a bright white explosion lights up the train beside her, the tracks, her beautiful face. And then she's gone. All that's left of our life together is one brown leather briefcase. Miraculously, they recovered her bloody leather briefcase. Everything else is gone in a flash of light. Brown eyes. Bright smile. Maggie. I can't save her.

"Mags, I love you!" I call out her name several times. In a sleepy fog, I hear someone screaming. Or is that me?

Twenty-nine

Hannah

I've been up since five a.m. No wonder, with Tripp's restlessness and nightmares. When he started screaming and breaking out into a sweat, I wanted to cry. It was painful to watch. I held him closer instead of running to the nearest exit like my instincts told me to. When he called out Maggie's name, I held his head close to my chest, kissed his forehead, and whispered, "It's okay, Tripp. I'm here." He finally stopped the screaming after a half hour, rolled out of my arms, and fell back into what looked like a peaceful slumber. I didn't sleep after that.

Now it's dawn, and sitting alone on the couch, tea in hand, Jughead resting in his cage and Coffee at my feet, things look different by morning light. Quite different.

He called out her name with me by his side. Maggie. He's still in love with her.

Everything feels wrong. Upside down. I gaze at the front page of the newspaper on the coffee table, its bold headline announcing the final day and night of the Cannes Film Festival. I used to attend that Festival with Doug every year. Whether he'd been in a film or not, he said it was crucial for him as an aspiring producer, to "make an appearance," and he always bought me a top of the line gown and diamond earrings for the VIP closing ceremony and after-party. I used to love being on his arm on that red carpet, knowing I had an exclusive ticket to one of the most talked about parties of the year. This was before I had my own TV series, and I remember feeling that, just by being on his arm, I was making all the right connections for my future.

I can't believe how being seen as "important" in social circles used to matter to me. One week here with Tripp, and I could not care less about attending some fancy film soirée. I'd rather spend the cost of a gown and ticket on fixing up Béa's place and helping to save the other run-down cottages along the shore. It took meeting someone who hasn't had anything handed to her on a silver platter to learn how simple it is for me to make a small difference in someone's life.

Tripp has taught me so much, and I love him. But am I seeing things clearly in this couple-bubble we've created? Yesterday, I was so happy here, playing with Tripp and our pets, ignoring the outside world. But the way Tripp just ignored my suggestion about becoming adoptive parents really threw me. It hurt. And yet, he definitely wants to foster the bird. Not Béa. I don't understand. I thought he loved her?

I swallow the last few drops of my tea and go over our conversation in my mind one more time. Oh, no. My realization makes me feel sick to my stomach.

It's not about Béa. It's about me. He doesn't want to be a parent with me because he doesn't see a future with me. This is just a fling. He's using me to get over Maggie. He never wanted this to be anything past the summer!

Could it really be that? No. I know this is more than a fling. We need to talk. I stand up, about to go wake Tripp and get this whole thing cleared up, when my phone buzzes. I grab it from the foyer table. I hope that it's Mom. She hasn't texted in days.

It's a text from Doug. I haven't heard from him since I asked if he could take care of Jughead while I was in France.

<Here at Cannes Festival. Your mom needs your help. I have a car out front to take you to us.>

I almost text back: <I'm not your wife anymore. I don't answer to you, and I never should have anyway!> but stop myself when I realize Mom could be in serious trouble.

<My mother is in Cannes?>

<No but have serious concerns about your mother and need to speak to you about that and the house sale. Meet me, and we can fly you back home quickly on my jet.>

<Can't you just tell me what's going on now?>

He doesn't answer, and I realize that my battery has died. I've been forgetting to check it, let alone plug it in, for days. I get up and open the front door. Just as Doug said, there's a man in a black suit in the driveway, standing beside a black limousine. He takes off his cap, holds it in both hands, and nods. I stare at the limo and am almost instantly transported back in time to my luxurious red-carpet days. It's bizarre to have that world waiting for me again, here on the doorstep of my island hideaway. I guess Jill isn't the best keeper of secrets after all.

God. Please let my mom be okay. If my ex is concerned about her, my ex who never worried about her in the past, what the hell is going on? My hands start to shake. I swallow back tears. Is that why she hasn't texted? Jill said Mom was concerned about me, but with everything going on here, I forgot to call her. I have a sinking feeling in my stomach and try not to pay any attention to it. I have to get out of here!

I search for the tote bag I was using yesterday. It's Tripp's, but he is happy to let me have it, for obvious reasons: It's bright red with bold white letters stating KEEP CALM AND LOVE PARROTS. I find it with my keys and credit cards, hanging beside the door, grab it and my dead phone, and begin to leave. Then I remember that Tripp is still asleep, and has no idea where I'm going, and I'm still in bare feet and my I NEED MY BEAUTY SLEEP nightshirt.

Oh, whatever! I can pull it off with a high ponytail and these black heels. I slip on the heels and look around to see if I'm forgetting anything else. The blue slicker. That would be helpful if it rains. I shove it inside the tote bag. There's no time to change or explain to Tripp why I've left. If I run upstairs and speak to him now, we'll have that whole awful-nightmare-he-was-screaming-he-loves-Maggie-doesn't-want-to-adopt-Béa conversation hanging over us like a heavyweight bag, and I just can't do that difficult talk right now. I'll text him. No, bad idea, he never checks messages!

I quickly scrawl, Needed to see Doug at Cannes festival. He says it's about my mom. Concerned. Will call soon. Love Hannah, on a piece of notepad paper and place it… where? I look around. Where will Tripp be sure to see it? He'll see it on Jughead's cage. I quickly place the note so it's jutting out from under the container of crackers. I can charge my phone at Doug's hotel and text or call Tripp with more details later.

As I close the door, fighting a gust of wind, I simultaneously pull my hair into a ponytail with the holder I had in my tote and pull down my I NEED MY BEAUTY SLEEP shirt as far as I can over my panties, so it looks like I meant to wear it as a dress. It falls just below my butt cheeks.

The limo driver puts his cap on and opens the door for me, but he gives me a funny look, and I know then and there that I can't pull this look off for the people at the Cannes Film Festival.

"Did you want to change? I can wait." The driver looks at me in the rear-view mirror.

I shake my head no, and he pulls the car out of the driveway. Who cares what they think? I'm doing this for Mom. They're all wannabe wankpuffins anyway.

The limo pulls up to a small red and black plane that's docked right beside where the ferry came in. I'm not a Wiki expert on seaplanes, but this looks sleek, sexy, and expensive. The limo driver is prattling on in broken English about how he's never seen anything like it.

"I saw it fly in like elegant bird with water skis. Two-seater. You have ride of lifetime!"

"Uh, okay," I say as I get out, and he quickly ushers me into the passenger seat of the plane. I'm feeling lightheaded and thinking how fast everything is moving and how I didn't ask for any of this.

I've never been in a small plane before. I buckle in, inhale deeply, and turn to the pilot for support, but I can't find his face. He's got blue mirror aviator sunglasses on, a large black headset and a microphone over his mouth. He gives me a nod.

Okay then. This is great. If this plane goes down, my final words ever will have been, "You bet, bud!" to a Hahn's mini macaw, who asked me first thing this morning, "Do you like piña coladas? Do you have half a brain?"

As the plane begins its ascent above the beautiful, lush island I've come to think of as home, I stare down at the dead phone in my hand, itching to get it charged almost as much as I'm itching to put on pants. I look down at the now-tiny island below us, searching for The Lighthouse, but I can't make anything out except a blur of coniferous green and ocean blue.

I try to sit back and enjoy my first ever seaplane flight, but my stomach is in knots. Am I doing the right thing? I had to find out what's going on with Mom and our house. There was no other way, with Doug being as controlling as ever. Tripp is probably reading my note right now. He'll find it, and he'll understand, and forgive me for leaving without saying goodbye.

As I think about it, I'm only five percent convinced, but my thoughts are suddenly interrupted by the realization that we've already landed, and the shocking sight of a large, excited crowd of people standing on the dock beside the plane.

Not just any people. Paparazzi.

Thirty

Tripp

"Han? You in the kitchen? You're not cooking for me, are you? Leave the spoiling to me. I like it."

I turn the living room corner and let my sentence trail off as I realize Hannah isn't anywhere in the house. I'm definitely alone. She must have gone for a walk, although, she usually needs a cup of tea or two before she's fully functional. I look around the room.

Oh. She's had tea. Empty cup right there on the coffee table. Newspaper, headline about the Cannes Film Festival, pencil and blank notepad… I look over to the door. Her shoes, the KEEP CALM AND

LOVE PARROTS tote I gave her, and her blue slicker are gone. Her phone isn't on the foyer table, either. Right then. Where's the note?

As I scan the bright, sunny room, Coffee strolls up to me, practically sits on my feet, and whimpers. She's clearly asking for food. "What's up sweets? Where'd Hannah go?" She whimpers again. I grab a couple of treats from the bag in the oak cabinet and feed them to Coffee.

"Yummy. Yummy for the tummy," Jughead squawks. He's moving his beak back and forth and spitting. Coffee runs to just below the cage and sniffs the floor.

"Coffee, stop licking the floor. C'mere girl." I grab her collar and make her lie at my feet as I sit down in my recliner. If she went for a walk, why didn't she leave me a note?

I try to remember our last words, but all I can recall is… oh bugger! I've scared her off. Oh, no. The nightmare about Maggie. I called out Maggie's name, I remember now. Hannah heard, in fact, she consoled me, held me, and when morning came, she decided she didn't want to put up with British Wussboy anymore.

Surely that's not it. She'd understand. We'd talk it out. We don't leave things unsaid. Especially not Hannah. I get up, grab my phone off the oak cabinet, slide it on, and start pacing by the window, hoping something will come to me, an idea, or a text.

A minute passes. I check the screen again. Come on Han, you didn't even text me? I check it once more.

"I realize I'm a bumbling naff of a Brit, and I don't have the phone attached to the palm of my hand like trending people do, but I do like to know where the bloody hell you are, because I love you. You have my heart, and now you have me all buggered, checking my bloody phone messages every five minutes!"

"Squawk!" Jughead bounces up and down on his perch, then throws up in his cage.

I stop pacing and glance at the cage. There's a white foamy mess below Jughead's perch. Ew. That's gross. Poor boy must have a little virus. Maybe ate some bad mango. But mango isn't white. I look a little closer. It's not just gross, it's Hannah's writing on white notepaper.

She did write me a note! And Jughead bloody ate it, the dim-witted numpty.

There are a couple pieces of paper left below the cage, where Coffee was sniffing earlier. I pick them up and try to make sense of them. They're just letters on tiny pieces of regurgitated paper. It's no use. I bend down so I'm at eye level with the macaw. "Alright, bird buddy, what did the bloody note say?" He just stares back at me, not even blinking. I grasp the rungs of the cage. "What did it bloody say?"

After another minute-long staring contest between man and green-eyed bird ensues from between the cage bars, I laugh out loud, realizing how ridiculous I must look and sound. I stand up and let my eyes scan the room. That blank pad on the coffee table. Right then! I could be like one of those old school detectives! She won't have to know about how panicked and pathetic I am that she's buggered off without leaving me a note, because I can decipher what she wrote. I grab the pencil, rip the last piece of paper out of the pad, and put it over the piece that was below her note. Alright, this should work just like a check book right? Carbon copy, here we come. I start scribbling over the paper.

I'd better keep my day job. It works nothing like I had anticipated, but I do make out a few words: Need see. Doug. festival.

Doug. She chose Doug.

"She went to the film festival with Doug, because she needed to? Couldn't we have gone together? Or, not at all, because those formal snobfests are for wankpuffins?"

Coffee stares up at me, cocks her head to the side, and whimpers. I toss the pencil across the room, throw the notepad down, stand up, and look around for something to kick. There's that copper basket full of wood at the corner of the hearth. I kick it as hard as I can.

Bloody hell! That hurt! I need to jump it out. I jump around, rubbing my left ankle with my hand, but I instantly fall over, landing like an elephant arse first.

"What the fuck!" Jughead's back to swearing again. He tilts his head and blinks at me. He looks pleased with himself.

Coffee comes right up to me and licks my forehead. I remain lying on my back, staring up at the ceiling. Good job with the British fury there, Wilson. That was real productive.

I sit up and look at Coffee. "Right, then. So, here's what I'm gonna do. I'm not gonna chase after her. She can be bloody well stay in Cannes for the rest of her life."

Coffee gives me her paw, and I shake it and slowly stand up. "Come on, girl, let's go for a ride in the truck. We have things to do."

Thirty-one

Hannah

The seaplane door opens, and I'm met with a giant gust of wind and saltwater mist spraying my face and hair. I take a strange man's hand and step gingerly, in three-inch black heels, from the plane to the dock. I almost lose my footing because I'm using my other hand to hold my KEEP CALM AND LOVE PARROTS tote against my hip in a miserable attempt to keep my nightshirt from flying up and over my ass.

I aced Film 404, but I fail one-hundred-percent in Don't Flash Your Ass At The Paparazzi. I wish I could recall what thong I wore today. I think it's the bright green one that says LUCKY ME, LUCKY YOU on it. This day just gets better and better.

Squawk! Squawk! Squawk! A flock of hungry sea gulls swarms overhead. I duck.

Click! Click! Click!

"Hannah, over here!"

And now, a swarm of prying eyes. I hear a scattering of words shouted my way.

"Neflix?" and "Pregnant?" and "Remarry?" Most of it is muffled by the wind, and I can't understand any of it, and besides, I've been trained not to answer.

The man who helped me off the plane has disappeared. I can't move forward, because I'm encircled by people holding cell phones or fancy wide lens cameras. No one is saying much anymore, they're just taking image after image of me in a flurry of excitement. I'm not sure where to turn, so I just put my hands on my hips like Doug taught me a decade ago, and force a wide, white smile for the cameras. I even give them a little wave, owning my odd appearance as best I can. My knee is aching already, and I've hardly walked anywhere. I'm so uncomfortable in these heels, and I already feel lost in this place. I'm someone else entirely now—a woman in patent leather heels, masquerading as the old me.

I continue posing for about a minute, but I'm quite sure they already got the money shot when I flashed them my LUCKY butt cheeks. I'm dying of embarrassment and wonder what shade of red my other cheeks are right now. I survey the crowd once more before moving forward. The seaplane has already started to drift away and is turning in the other direction. Back to the island? I feel a pang in my heart, and my left knee buckles a little beneath me. I'd almost forgotten that it's still bandaged. I overhear some paparazzi desperate for a story adding hearsay about that into the mix of words being shouted my way.

"Accident?"

"Beaten!"

"Marital abuse!"

Suddenly, I realize I don't have any allies here. Not one. And zero security.

Someone should be greeting me, protecting me from this mob. Why isn't Doug here, or Jill, or at the very least one of his security people? And why is this crowd even interested in me? I haven't been the talk in television for six months now.

I try to regain my balance and look to the right, and the paparazzi turn and start photographing what I'm looking at. If they think photos of cabs and that little electric bus will excite their readers, more power to them. I'm trying to decide which way to walk. I know from the Google maps walking trips I tried on the plane that I'm looking over at the oldest part of town, Le Suquet, an area with narrow streets, a medieval church, and a twelfth century castle. I've always wanted to go see that church and castle, and I'm tempted to do exactly that and never bother with meeting Doug, but I desperately need to talk to Mom. I need to charge this phone!

I take a step to the left, which I know is the beautiful Boulevard de la Croisette, lined with luxury hotels. The minute I step off the dock, the entire pack begins to follow me. This is ridiculous. I'm that chicken crossing the road, and they're the chicks. What will I get on the other side?

A woman with bulging eyes and buzzed, platinum-blonde hair holding a clipboard against her chest rushes up to my side and grabs me at the elbow. She starts walking me away from the water toward the bustling city streets.

"Hannah. I'm Joyce, Doug's publicist. He couldn't make it to the dock, but he's waiting for you at the Palais des Festivals, where all the action is. He should just be starting lunch now. Let's get you… er… cleaned up. You'll be dining with VIP." She nods at my nightshirt and tote and turns her head away towards the ocean, like she can't stomach what she sees.

"Madame, venez avec moi." A limo driver in a dark suit appears out of nowhere beside Joyce and holds out his arm for me, as if he's my French knight in shining armor. A little too late dude, the whole world just saw my Canadian ass in all its glory.

"Your mister awaits you," he says firmly and takes my elbow, pushing me towards the waiting black stretch limo.

"He's not my mister. If he were, he'd have met me here." I wriggle out of his grip and turn to Joyce. "I can walk or take the bus. I'm fine!" Joyce is already sliding into the backseat.

The limo driver scowls at me. I suppose he won't get his tip if I don't get in. Joyce glares up at me; red faced, with those bulging eyes.

"Hannah, for fuck sake, just get in. People don't keep Doug Evan waiting."

She looks like she's going to pop a vein in her neck. I bite my lower lip and stare out at the calming sea, weighing my options. An angry driver and an overworked publicist, or a pack of hungry paparazzi? I look back at the restless crowd. I am afraid for my life around these crazy paparazzi people. I decide to play it safe and get in the back of the limo beside Joyce.

"Good girl. You made the right choice." She offers me a fake smile, complete with a chunk of red lipstick on her left front tooth. I look down at my lap and snicker to myself, feeling amused for the first time all morning. She condescends me with "good girl;" I'm not going to tell her about the lipstick.

I hear a phone buzz, and my heart flutters, until I realize it can't be my phone. Joyce glances at her sleek gold-covered device. "Change of plans. Doug will be returning to the Festival later. He's at his hotel, dining on the rooftop at Restaurant Le 360. He says to join him there."

The limo makes a quick turn. I look out the window and see people shopping, talking, and laughing in the midday sun. Of course. It's a gorgeous day in the Mediterranean, and I'm stuck inside this car, about to have a forced lunch with my ex. I feel so trapped. He texted his publicist, but he didn't feel he owed me an explanation for not meeting me at the dock? I bet when I charge my cell, I'll discover that he didn't text. What a jerk.

I open my tote and check my phone, as if looking at it will revive it from the dead. I need to charge it or use the phone in the hotel to call Mom. How can Doug be enjoying a rooftop lunch when his ex-mother-in-law isn't well? Something isn't right about any of this. "I need to make an important phone call. Can we use Doug's room before I meet with him?"

"No Hannah, he's on a tight schedule." Joyce purses her lips. "Perhaps you can use his phone once you sit down with him." She stares at me a moment, then takes a nail file from her clutch purse and starts filing her pinky nail. "I can only hope people will assume your outfit is a Canadian fashion statement."

I want to use the B word right now to her face, but Tripp's soothing voice comes to mind. "She's a total wankpuffin. Ignore her." Suddenly, I feel at ease, and confident enough to grill her for more information.

"Why were the paparazzi all over me back there? Doug was always the rising star. I was just his writer wife. The TV show did well enough in its heyday, but it's over now. Why were they so interested in me?"

Her jaw drops, and she puts down her nail file. "You honestly have no idea?"

"No idea about what?"

"Hashtag Douannah, honey. It's lit or bit or a hit. Whatever the lingo is today, that hashtag has gone viral practically overnight! You two are the talk of the town. It's the most brilliant move of my career."

"You? You started it?" I can feel my chest, neck, and ears growing hot with anger. Wonderful. Let's add "splotchy-chest" to my list of fashion faux-pas.

"It was just one innocent little tweet, honey, suggesting you two were back on. I never expected the public to latch onto the story like they have." She smiles, claps her hands together, and squeals, as if we're the next Brad and Jen, Justin and Selena, Harry and Meghan. I just want to be Tripp and Hannah, in a forest where nobody knows our names!

"But it's not true!" I shout.

"True, shmoo." She rolls her eyes. "What's truth got to do with anything anymore, sweetheart? This is big business. In one month, your old show has spiraled to the number one spot on Netflix. All thanks to one little tweet. The public has spoken. They want you two together."

I feel faint. "Let me out." I say firmly but calmly, flicking the button on my door back and forth. It doesn't open. I raise my voice. "Let. Me. Out!"

She motions to the driver to pull over. "Calm down, Ginger!" She frowns at me. "Doug told me you were feisty, but I didn't think I'd have to babysit you this entire time."

"If you don't let me out, I'll make a public statement that I was kidnapped at Cannes by Doug and his publicist."

"You'll sound completely batty but go ahead." She sighs and tells the driver to let me out, pushes a button to slide down the window, and shoves some fifty-dollar bills at the valet without even speaking to him. He grabs the money and starts to open the car door for her. "We're already at the hotel anyway, Hannah. I'll show you the way to the restaurant."

"Thanks, but no thanks." I slam the limo door. "I don't need any of you wankpuffins helping me."

Joyce looks confused about what I've said, then seconds later, as if she's finally realized it was an insult, gives me the finger through the open door. The valet looks at her, then looks me up and down, smiles with amusement, and opens the heavy hotel door for me.

What do you know? I didn't even tip him, and I got service before Joyce. It makes me chuckle. I slip into the hotel lobby before any paparazzi notice me and look around for the nearest gift shop.

I can handle Doug the Slug, anytime, anywhere. But I need to be wearing pants.

Thirty-two

Hannah

The black leggings are itchy and barely fit around my bandaged knee. I just wanted to wear jogging pants, but the leggings and a fitted pink CANNES IS FOR LOVERS t-shirt were all the gift shop had left in my size. With my red locks in a high ponytail and several bangle bracelets on my wrist to tie the outfit together, I'm more of a Fashion Yay than the Fashion Nay I was down at the dock, but I also look about eighteen. I'm sure Doug and his business buddies, who always turn out to be more like frat brothers, will absolutely love that. I don't want to be doing him any favors.

Coming here pantless was bad enough, but I can't believe I didn't think to grab my powerpack before leaving The Lighthouse. I can't believe I was stupid enough to leave The Lighthouse. Tripp would say I've been a dim-witted numpty, and he'd be half-right. If I can just borrow Doug's phone and speak with Mom, I can sort this whole fiasco out.

I step off the elevator and look around Le 360's rooftop patio. There are about twenty occupied tables with beautiful lime green fabric chairs and hot pink peony bouquets at their center. The tables are shaded with large, crisp white umbrellas. Each table has a 360-degree view of Cannes and the sparkling teal blue ocean. I'd be hanging over the glass balcony, snapping photos and drooling over the aesthetic if I didn't have more serious matters to attend to.

It doesn't take long for me to find Doug. I hear his faux, self-confident, booming laughter first. It echoes from his table at the center of the patio all the way across the roof to where I'm standing. Within seconds, my presence is noticed, and we're both turning heads and gathering whispers. "Doug Evan," a man at the corner table stage-whispers to his companion, and she quickly takes her phone out of her purse. Then her eyes meet mine. She starts to pan the cell phone my way, but I frown at her and shake my head. "Please, no," I mouth. She looks down at her Greek salad, embarrassed. I think she's a teenage celebrity, but I can't remember her name. It's getting weird now. Celebrities are fangirling over me. I didn't ask for this!

I walk briskly over to Doug's table and hang my tote over an empty chair, saying nothing. He raises his dark eyebrows, lowers his sunglasses, and grins up at me, but he doesn't get up.

"Hani! So glad you could join us. Sexy outfit, babe. You always had style."

"Babe?" I breathe in through my teeth so they almost whistle, trying not to shout at him. I know I must remain calm, but I'm going to fail miserably. "Why did you ask me here, Doug? What's going on with Mom?" As I cross my arms over my chest and look to my left, I notice someone filming us. Not with a cell phone, but with a large film production camera. A short, stocky man is holding the camera and a taller one is holding an umbrella. At first, I thought it was another patio umbrella, but now I can tell it's for lighting.

"What's going on?" I lower my voice and glare at him.

"Sit down," he says, and I do so, not to follow his orders, but because I want the cameraman to stop zooming in on my legs, ass, and ankles.

"These camera guys follow me everywhere, now. I'll explain in a minute." He motions to three bearded men at the table who are wearing expensive caramel colored suits and blue shirts identical to his and raises a pint of beer.

"Gentlemen, this is my Hannah." He adjusts his dark sunglasses, pushing them back on his nose. "I just had a private Ace five-forty seaplane pick her up while we were having drinks. Didn't want to interrupt our business but had to please the little lady, as well." He leans back in his chair. "Dropped a few thousand Francs. What are you gonna do?" He smiles wide, and they all laugh and nod in agreement, like he's given a stellar State of the Union address, and they'll be breaking out the whiskey and cigars any minute.

I roll my eyes. He doesn't see me at all. He begins cutting his filet mignon as he plays to his posse. "I just rented the seaplane, of course. The one I took across the Atlantic is mine. It's new this year. Even has a three-piece bedroom in it." The men keep staring and smiling at him like he's a World Series game and they can't miss one play. I want to puke.

"Doug. The cameras. Tell them to leave." I say it firmly but low, aware of the dozens of pairs of eyes on me.

He ponders this for a moment, then waves the cameramen away. In an instant, they're gone, and onlookers in the restaurant start to return to their own business. I move onto private matters.

"What's going on with Mom? Is she okay? Is she in hospital?"

"Ah, that." Doug sighs, his dark eyes narrowing. He takes his fork and uses it to carefully scrape out pieces of corn from the cob on his plate. He eats four kernels slowly, meticulously. He's going to take an hour to eat his forking corn. I'm still waiting for an answer when he slowly puts his fork down beside his steak and takes a long swallow of beer. The three men with him follow suit. They're all eating their corn exactly the same way. I blink. Then I blink once more and shake my head, hoping that the rattling will wake me from this bad dream.

"Hani," Doug finally responds, "I found your Mom at our place, lounging by the pool, drinking pineapple mojitos with some man I've never met. Highly inappropriate, if you ask me."

What the hell were you doing there? I nearly scream. I glare at him. "Our place! Our place isn't our place since I kicked you out! I asked Mom to stage it for the showings." I'm livid that he interfered like this. I can't believe he kept his key.

"Damnit, where's a good pineapple mojito when you need one?" I put my hands in my head and exhale, then turn to him, grab his beer and take a long swig. He doesn't look surprised. He knows me, and he knows that he's been playing with fire. What I can't figure out is why. What does he want from me?

"Well, you didn't tell me that, sweetheart." He looks at each of his friends and shakes his head. "Women!" They all laugh. One raises his beer. I scowl at him, and he shrinks a little in his seat and immediately puts it down.

"So, Mom doesn't need my urgent help?"

"Personally, I think she needs psychiatric help. She told me she wants to buy the place. She asked the realtor to take it off the market this week."

I look down at the plate in front of me and feel a wave of relief wash over me. She's not in hospital. She's met someone. I can't wait to hear about him. It's been at least a decade since she dated anyone, and I want her to be happy. "Sounds like a Mom move to me! I'd love to sell her the house. I'm sure she was going to tell me soon, but I've been a little preoccupied—there was a flood where I was staying, and we helped some people out and..."

"Yes, yes, yes." He's not even listening; he's reading his phone. A second later he looks up and over at me. "You look… different." He removes his sunglasses and finally takes a moment to look at me. "What happened to your knee? Whatever have you been doing on that odd little island over there, Hani?"

"Stop calling me that!" I finish his beer, slamming the glass on the table. "I want to know why you summoned me here like some kind of king, when Mom's doing just fine, and the house isn't on fire. What the hell is going on?"

"Sorry, can't explain that now, doll." He's reading another text that just came in. He throws his napkin down and stands, and the men with him stand and do the same. He motions for someone to come over to the table, and to my shock, Joyce appears from behind a tall plant in the corner of the room. She hands me a black garment bag.

"Wear the dress. I'm booked solid in meetings until four p.m.," Doug says, still staring at his phone. "But there's a cocktail party before the closing ceremonies, and I can sit down with you then and explain everything." He lowers his glasses. "Hani. You need to hear what I have to propose. Trust me. I'll leave some security detail with you."

"Damnit, Doug just tell me now!" I want to scream. I'm not sure what newfound strength inside me—the island?—is keeping me still, but I manage to say it firmly, not loudly.

"Doug. You're already fifteen minutes late," Joyce hisses as she grabs his elbow and begins to steer him towards the elevator.

Doug shrugs his shoulders at me. "It is what it is. What are ya gonna do? See you at four, babe." He and Joyce rush out of the room, followed by his three colleagues. I'm left standing by the table holding up a garment bag.

"Hello, Hannah Storm. We heard you say pineapple mojito?" A tall waiter approaches me and gives me a smile. He's holding up a yellow drink garnished with a slice of pineapple and a tiny green umbrella. "This one's pineapple vanilla, compliments of the manager."

Okay then, clearly there are some benefits to my silly newfound fame. I thank him as I take the refreshing-looking drink from his hand, hang the garment bag over a chair, and flop back down at the table. I exhale deeply, not caring who hears.

One of the two security men who had been standing behind the camera people pulls up a chair beside me. He's got streaks of sweat running down his cheekbones, and his shaved head has been sunburned. His steel-blue eyes tell me he's tired and feeling old, yet I'd say he's about my age, maybe a couple years younger. Is he tired of the gig, or tired of the people?

"Security." He smiles at me and puts out his hand. He leans in a little and whispers, "But if you wanna be human about it, call me Hank.'" I laugh at the way he deadpans that. I take his outstretched hand and shake it.

"I'm Hannah."

"So, I hear you're from Canada? Always wanted to go. Beautiful country. Bloody love your Prime Minister's socks."

His knowledge of Canada and his strong British accent make me grin right back at him. I can't believe this. It's like Tripp truly is sending me love messages from across the ocean. Maybe he got my note. Maybe we're all good, and I don't have to worry. I still have to get my phone charged so I can speak to him and Mom.

Hank puts on his sunglasses and stares out at the sea, and I realize that I feel safe for the first time since I arrived in Cannes. Maybe he can help me out of this colossal mess.

"Bottoms up," I say. I raise my glass to my funny new friend and down the drink.

Thirty-three

Hannah

"You look like something the feral cat dragged in."

"Gee, thanks Mom. Not just a cat. A feral one. Nice." My mother's beautiful, slender image has just appeared on Hank's phone, which he kindly loaned to me.

I stretch my legs out on the bed's quilted, dark grey duvet. Doug's penthouse corner suite has it all: King bed, a wet bar, a jacuzzi tub in the corner, wall to ceiling glass windows, and a glass paneled balcony with sweeping ocean views. I remember living like this whenever Doug took me to LA on business, which was, now that I think of it… only once. I got sunstroke, and we bickered the entire time.

I study my Mom's face. It's lightly tanned and healthy-looking, but small and pixelated. Her floppy, pristine, white sunhat shades her grey-blue eyes, exposing a few wrinkles at their corners. She's officially a senior now, but she hasn't looked this good in years. She looks well-rested and happy.

I stare at her for a moment. She's too far from me—a whole sea and ocean away. I wish she could give me a hug right now. You're never too old for a mom hug. You're never too old to hear her tell you, "everything is going to be okay."

"Well, you're so pale, and you know I don't like your hair in a ponytail. It's too frizzy like that—it's so sleek and pretty when you wear it down. And whose number is this anyways? I almost didn't answer, but you called three times." She's wearing a hot pink one-piece swimsuit, and that's my pool in the background, but I'm okay with her being there. She changed my diapers, nursed me, held me until I finally fell asleep every night for a year after Dad died. She deserves to take a dip in my swimming pool whenever she darn well wants.

"This is my friend Hank's phone." Hank leans over the bed, and, though I'm sure he intends to smile with his whole face, reveals only his bald sunburned head and bushy eyebrows to my Mom. He raises his eyebrows and says a jovial, "Hello there, Mrs. Hannah."

Mom blushes and lies back in her lounge chair.

"Oh, my!" She giggles. As Hank walks back to the room's elaborate wet bar, his back turned to me, she lowers her voice and whispers. "He's very big! I hope when he's with you that he's gentle…"

I cut her off. "Mother!" I roll my eyes. "He's not my boyfriend. He's a security guard here at the hotel, and he was put on Doug's detail for the week, but he wants to quit."

"Who wouldn't want to quit working for Doug? Oh. That bastard was here, by the way." She frowns.

"I know Mom, that's why I'm calling! He had me worried sick about you."

"Oh, what did he go and tell you, now? That man. Lies, lies, lies."

"He made me think you might be in hospital. That's why I rushed here, to have him fly me to you. So, you're fine?"

"Sweetheart I'm better than fine. You won't believe it. I've met the most incredible man." She sighs and starts to fan herself. "Cruz is tall, tanned, and Spanish. He's so full of energy. We're taking Salsa lessons together. He's just out getting us something to eat."

Cruz? He sounds at least a decade younger. Go, Mom! "That's fantastic. Me too! I mean, I've met someone too. He's definitely not a salsa-dancing Spaniard." I chuckle. "He's a bird-studying Brit. And he's absolutely wonderful."

"So that's who you've been up to!" Mom laughs. "I knew you were happy. You don't need me as much when you're happy." She sighs, but she looks serene as she says it.

"I can't wait to talk about your new man more, but I think I have to go beat up my ex-husband." I frown, furrowing my brow dramatically as if I'm three years old again.

She looks at me and shakes her head. "Don't beat him up. Beat him at his own game."

I raise an eyebrow. She has a point.

"I think you're right. Before I go, Mom… did you really ask the realtor to take the house off the market?"

"What? No! Did Doug lie about that, too?"

"Yup." I sigh.

"I told him I was waiting to ask you," she says. "I do love this place… seems a pity to let it leave the family…"

"Sold. Tell the agent we're doing a private sale. I'll vid you later, maybe tomorrow."

"You make fast decisions in your older age…" She smiles at me.

"I didn't always, but I finally know what I want. And Mom… I need to go before I lose it!" I blow her a kiss.

"Bye dear." She raises a mojito in the air, and it makes me grin.

I turn the video call off and hand the phone back to Hank, who takes it and offers me a pineapple mojito. He's been making me snacks and drinks over at the wet bar.

"Oh, I don't think I should have another drink. These are pretty strong."

"I'll watch over you. I overheard what Doug did to you. Worrying you like that for no good reason! You'll need liquid courage for your meeting with him." He leaves the drink on the wet bar, just in case I change my mind, turns a brown leather chair towards the bed and sits down.

I look up at the closed garment bag hanging in the closet. Hank is just staring at it, too. It's a star in a universe that neither of us wants to explore anymore. But, it's there, beckoning us. It's hard to ignore. What do we do with it?

"So," I walk over to the bag and start to unzip it. "You still convinced I should go to this party?"

Thirty-four

Hannah

Hank sits back and puts his feet up on the ottoman. "I don't know… Doug has some kind of television deal lined up for you, right?"

"Something like that." I crouch down as I continue unzipping the garment bag. "I need to at least find out what the terms are. From the sounds of it, it's a lot of money. I probably shouldn't pass it up…"

Hank crosses his arms over his chest, frowning. "It's really none of my business…" His voice trails off, and I realize that he isn't sure if he should continue to be so candid.

I stop what I'm doing for a second and stand up. "No, go ahead. I'd love your opinion."

"I've been watching that guy the past twenty-four hours, strutting his stuff like he owns the hotel. He comes off like a complete phony. I don't get why you'd want to work with him."

"Well, I don't." I toss the bag over the back of the other leather chair and begin pacing the floor. "I just thought I should hear him out. Hear what he has to offer."

"What he has to offer?"

"His business was my business for over ten years, and walking away from it all, forever, well, it's just not the easiest thing to do…" I choke back tears. This is it. I'm really going to walk away from a career I spent over a decade building.

It's not about the money, or the fame, because that's all so fleeting, and not important in the end. It's all of the time and energy I've invested. It's hard to accept, but I need to put it all behind me. I'm going to have to look at my sitcom work not as a loss, but as a stepping stone that took me to where I want to be. I'm a different woman now, with new goals. I can't keep writing fiction when there's so much truth to be told.

"If it makes it easier, I'll walk away with you." Hank says. "I'd love to see the island and meet the people you've been talking about."

I stare at him. "You're going to quit the VIP security business, just like that?"

"Just like that." He reaches over to a pizza box on the table and grabs a large slice of the Hawaiian he ordered for us. It's from some place down the street. I found it funny when he didn't want a single item on the room service menu. He doesn't fit in with this whole scene, either.

"I don't like these people," he says, as if confirming my thoughts, "and I don't like living here. Sometimes new adventures beckon, and you have to leap and figure out how you'll land while you're still up in the air."

I grab the garment bag and fully open it, revealing a stunning strapless gown inside. It's a beautiful, deep forest green color with thousands of sparkling diamond studs decorating the bodice and a fitted mermaid style skirt that flares out just below the knee. I stare at the dress, breathless for a moment, but all I can think about is Tripp's forest. Our forest.

I turn to Hank. "Can you help me get out of Cannes without a scene? Protect me from the paparazzi?"

"I sure can try," he says. "I know a few back streets, and we can slip onto the five o'clock ferry as it leaves."

His plan makes me smile. "You seemed so serious, a little conservative because of your job, but you're actually spontaneous!"

"I can be." Hank grins.

"Well, if you're up for a new adventure, you're in luck. I happen to know someone who might need your muscles, at least for the summer. And your brains, of course—I wouldn't want to treat you like a piece of British Beefcake." I smile at him.

"Beefcake, ha!" He chuckles. "Yeah, a lot of the VIP ladies here treat me like that. One even shoved a fiver down my pants. Was quite dismayed she didn't think I was worth more."

I bite my lower lip. He's easy on the eyes, but I'm not about to say it.

"So," he leans forward with interest, "we're talking construction work on the island? Sounds..." As he begins to ask me more, my phone buzzes on the bedside table.

"It's charged! It's charged!" I squeal. I resist the urge to wrap my arms around him to thank him for loaning me his charger. It feels like we're best buds already, but I'm not sure how he'd react to a hug from me yet, and besides, he's got a bad case of pizza-sauce hands.

My phone's screen displays a couple notifications, but the only one I truly care about is a text from Tripp, sent ages ago.

<You okay? Surprised you just left like that but giving you your space. Here for you.>

My heart skips a beat. He's here for me. I knew that. I felt it this entire time. But he thinks I need space! This is not good. So not good. I mean, it's lovely that I've met a man mature enough to realize people sometimes need space in a relationship, but that's not what this is! I don't want space; I want to be drinking tea with him, naked in bed! I need to clear this up...

"Go call your man." Hank sees the conflicted look on my face and smiles up at me, then bites into another slice of pizza. "I'll clean up in here and wait for you to get ready to leave. I have a feeling this is going to be a night to remember."

I take my tote, dress, and phone and walk to the large bathroom, closing the door but leaving it slightly ajar so that steam can escape. Once inside, I look once more at the glimmering dress in my hand. I'm sure it's worth thousands. I'm curious, will it look good on me? I'll slip it on before I shower just for the fun of it. I whip off my t-shirt and leggings, take the dress out of the bag and pull it on. It's a tight-fitting mermaid skirt, but the style suits my figure, and I feel glamorous. I zip it up as far as I can at the back, then look at my sexy reflection and twirl in a circle to take a peek at my behind. Seconds later, I nearly lose my balance and need to grab the counter for support.

"Ugh!" It happens so fast, I can only grunt my embarrassment.

"You okay, Hannah?" Hank calls to me.

"Fine, fine, just, uh, gas." Gas? That was smooth. Maybe I'd better just stick to the original plan.

I grab my phone off the counter, sit on the soaker tub's wide edge, and start to compose a text to Tripp. I stop when I hear someone entering the room and a voice I would know anywhere. It's my best friend, Jill.

"Oh Hank, sexy Hank, here you are. Is it your b-b-b-break?" She giggles. It's not just Jill, it's drunk Jill. I know that giggle well.

"I was hoping you'd join me at the cocktail party. Doug is always so busy at these things…" I hear some rustling, but I can't figure out what's going on. I quickly hide behind the bathroom door, in case Jill comes in.

I look down at my feet. Doug is always so busy at these things. That sounded so… familiar. Like she's at Doug's side all the time.

"Uh, yeah, I'm just here… chilling…" Hank sounds uncomfortable, and I can tell immediately from his tone that Jill has no idea I'm here. I stay hidden.

"Did you see the scene Doug's ex made up at Le 360? Did you? What time is it, four? She's at the cocktail party with him, now. He invited her! I am so jealous that he has eyes for her again. And let's not get started on that ridiculous Douannah hashtag!"

Jealous? Jill? But… she hates Doug. She always said so.

"I don't think you should be on my lap, and we shouldn't be talking about…" Hank sounds extremely nervous, too nervous to reveal that I'm in the bathroom. I understand now how it could look like we were together intimately in this room, not just two people getting to know one another. He's young, this was his first security job, and we both know that he was supposed to stand outside the door. He still feels a sense of responsibility to the work. I'm certain that he wants to leave on his own terms, not because one of his bosses discovers he's been up to no good with me in a hotel room.

"Did you see the atrocity that Hannah called an outfit?" I'm pretty sure Hank just lifted her off his lap, but I peek through the crack between the wall and the door to verify my theory. Jill is barely standing, bracing herself on Hank's chair, stumbling over her feet and her words.

"Did you see that ass in those leggings?" Jill continues. "She's gotten a wee bit plumpers, is that how the British say it? Why does the paparazzi make such a big fuss over her? Well. Whatevs." She exhales loudly. "Doug always preferred me naked anyway."

I hear it, but it doesn't quite register. I need time to process it.

Doug always preferred Jill naked.

I slump to the bathroom floor. I can't feel my legs. My whole body feels numb. My heart is racing and pounding in my ears. I might throw up. Thankfully, there's a toilet right beside me if I decide that I need to.

Just then, my phone buzzes, and I quickly grab it off the counter and switch it to silent so that Jill doesn't hear it. I need to stay hidden and listen more. I don't want to hear about how my husband and best friend deceived me. How many times? How many years? I don't want to, but I need to.

I look down at my phone, my eyes brimming with tears. There's a new notification on the front screen. I wipe my eyes as the first of what I imagine will be thousands of tears fall. To my surprise, I find myself laughing inside my mind. What I'm reading is very funny, in a cruel, twisted way. It's a message from Good Nights.

<How would you rate your stay? Please complete our short online survey!>

I tap to open the Good Nights app and notice that the time and date are no longer frozen. Everything is back to normal now that I'm off the island and in Cannes, but nothing feels normal here in this place, with these people. Everything feels fast-paced, upside down, and wrong.

Rate my stay, you ask? I close my eyes, remembering Tripp's and my tandem bike ride, our intimate dinner, that sensual bubble bath fight, making love by the light of kerosene lamps. It was five brilliant stars, the most amazing stay of my entire life, even though you idiots double-booked us! I find myself smiling, and a wave of warm love washes over me. My hands are shaking, and my heart is still pounding in my ears, but I know that I'm going to be okay. Everything will be okay, in time.

I close the app and text Tripp.

<Coming home to The Lighthouse tonight.>

There. That should do it. Then, just in case, I send one more text: <Love you!>

I slide the phone off, put it inside my tote, and force myself to listen to what my drunk and lying ex-best friend is saying in the other room.

Thirty-five

Hannah

"So…" Hank sounds like he's about to throw up, too.

"Jill. Baby."

I know intuitively that Jill is not Hank's baby. He's on my side. He wants me to hear the truth, and he's saying whatever he needs to say to get a confession for me. I knew it the moment he stepped forward to keep me company on that lonely rooftop patio: Hank has my back.

"I was wondering what this big offer Doug has for Hannah is all about?" he asks.

"Oh yes, that." Jill sounds bored already. She prefers talking about herself, I suppose. "Well Doug wanted her here, you know, to get publicity for the new show he shopped to the network. It's about their life and challenges as writers and performers. The Write Way: Doug and Hannah. I mean it's reality, but embellished reality, so I get to write stuff, make stuff up. I'm so psyched!"

Embellished reality? About me and Doug? How can she even imagine that I'd be on board with this? Who is this woman who used to be my best friend, and what have they done with her brain? I sneak another peek through the gap between the door and wall again. Hank's expression looks a lot like mine. As Tripp would say, he's completely gobsmacked.

"So, you two coerced Hannah here to parade her around for a reality show that's not even sold yet?" His mouth is open, and he looks incredulous. It seems he can't even look at her now; he's turned his back to her, and he's looking out the window.

"Tiny details, my friend, small details, never you mind." She is so condescending. She walks up to him and puts her arms around his waist from behind, but he instantly pulls them off. She keeps yammering, regardless. "Hannah's old show on Netflix is the bomb since Joyce's tweet went viral. This new show will be a hit. Total hit. You know what, sexy? You should come along to L.A., work as our security. I'm sure Doug could get you in. He's already said that I can be head writer. We just need her to sign on as a co-producer, and you know, to let us film them as they go about their LA days, for the ratings. It's the only way George at the network wants the show... with the fallout after their divorce and everything."

She finally stops talking to take breath. Then she begins to laugh. "It's the motus opera in Hollywood today. Disaster sells well."

"I think you mean modus operandi." I hear total annoyance in Hank's tone.

"Whatevs. It's like, how we do things now, according to George," Jill says.

George, CEO of my old network. I exhale, clenching my fists and trying not to punch a hole in the bathroom door. Of course, George is behind this! Of course. Those three deserve one another.

So, Jill is not only disloyal, she's also a suck-up and a brainless follower. She'll copy whatever everyone else is doing, even if it's wrong, as long as it gets her to the top. I've heard more than enough. I'm getting out of here, and I won't let her see my tears.

I wipe my wet eyes with the back of one hand, pull my hair out of its ponytail and give it a shake so it falls naturally over my shoulders, then glance in the mirror. There. I may not be the most glamourous woman at this party, but at least I'll be me. I would be more me if I were wearing my favorite pair of army green wellies, and what an appearance that would be! Oh well. The heels in the closet by the door will have to suffice, although they're starting to pinch my toes.

I take a step back from the mirror, and my tote accidentally hits the door, making it creak.

"Who… who's there?" Jill is standing outside the bathroom door.

"Your best friend since junior high." I walk out and confront her. "Well, not so much anymore, you gormless, people-pleasing wankpuffin."

She looks confused at the onslaught of strange words, which completely amuses me. Then she pouts and opens her arms as though she expects me to walk into her pathetic apology hug. "Oh, Hannah, honey."

I cross my arms over my chest and I don't move forward.

She looks surprised that I'm standing here in front of her, quite upset. "Darling, you weren't supposed to get hurt. You weren't supposed to ever know about us…"

I don't think she's rattled because she has hurt me. She lied to me once in high school about copying my science project idea, and she has the same look on her face now that she had when I confronted her about that. She's been caught in a web of lies, and she's only flustered because she promised Doug she'd keep their affair under wraps. Now he'll be angry with her, and I am all too familiar with Doug's volatile nature.

"You're the brunette." I glare at her. It's not a question.

"I am. Yes. I am. Oh, Hani. We didn't mean for it to happen…" She finally drops her arms to her side.

"Sure. It sounds like an honest mistake."

She hears the sarcasm in my voice and looks over her shoulder at Hank, hoping for an ally in this standoff. He's sitting in a chair by the wet bar, putting on his black leather shoes.

I look at my old friend and quickly realize that I'm not even angry at her. I simply pity her. I pity her for falling for Doug the Slug and his every façade. She has no idea who he really is. "You know, back when I was creating my show, people whispered behind my back that Doug was sneaking around with a brunette," I say. "I didn't want to hear it, didn't want to believe it. Besides, I figured if it was true, it was someone from out of town. Maybe a woman he met in New York. I didn't think it could be as simple as scrolling through my contacts list."

"Hannah-banana… sweetheart… I'm sorry." She hasn't called me that since seventh grade. She reaches out to touch my left shoulder, and I back away.

"Oh no. No. Don't touch me. There's no fixing this," I say.

She rolls her eyes, then stares at a broken fingernail on her left hand. She's exhausted every bit of empathy that she could muster for me from inside her cold, calculating heart. Now she wants to focus on her manicure. "I suppose you're going to throw a glass of water in my face, now, huh?" she asks.

I shake my head as I walk over to the wet bar and stand beside Hank, who gets up for me.

"No. No that would be too predictable. Far too Hollywood," I say.

She blinks at me, clueless, as Hank hands me a full glass. I look at it and grin.

"I'm going to pour a pineapple mojito over your head. Much more satisfying."

I pour the entire drink over her hair, slowly, with a few little hand flourishes, like a master chef marinating a steak, tossing the pineapple wedges and two cherries at her dress as I leave the room. They mostly land in her cleavage.

"Oh! You! That's… this is… so gross!" Jill is screeching, dripping wet, and trying to pull chunks of fruit from her chest.

"Oh, and something I should warn you about," I pull my tote high on my shoulder, slip on my heels, then stop at the doorframe and turn back to her, "don't ever tell Doug he's not right, about anything. He'll smash something valuable. Have fun with that. Bye now."

Hank gives me his right arm, and I take it. We can't contain our laughter as we enter the elevator together. He's making snort noises. The couple inside stare at us. I don't care. I feel fantastic.

"How did you know?" I ask when I finally compose myself. "To hand me the drink?"

"I didn't, it just felt so right." He smiles. "I'm never going to forget that look of horror on her face!" He throws back his head and starts laughing again. The couple in the elevator are staring at their feet, trying to avoid our eyes.

"We still making an appearance at the cocktail party?" Hank asks as we reach the hotel lobby and exit the elevator.

"Nope. I've changed my mind." I'm still holding onto his right arm and feel him veering gently down a hallway I didn't know about, toward a lone back door.

"Doug wants a scene," I say, pulling out a blue "CANNES" cap from my tote and slipping it on my head. "That's why he brought me here. Any footage of me getting angry at him is good publicity for him. Or, worse, he'll find a way to use it for the show I'm not signing up for. I won't give him the satisfaction. I'm walking away."

"Just like that?" Hank sounds proud of me. He squeezes the top of my hand, then pulls his shades over his eyes as he opens the back door for me, and we walk out into the late afternoon sun.

"Just like that," I say.

"Besides," I add. "I need to get home."

Thirty-six

Hannah

The ocean is a sparkling blue oasis calling my name. I can see the way to it, just past a straight row of palm trees one street over. We'd be in good shape, maybe even sitting on that ferry right now, if I could waddle in this mermaid skirt any faster than the snail's pace I'm currently moving at.

"Do you think you could have worn something slightly more practical for an escape to the island?" Hank says. He can't seem to contain his laughter. Of course, he's all set for our getaway and looking the part of a handsome young spy in shades, black pants and fitted black t-shirt. I'm quite a different story. I've got my bright blue slicker on over the strapless green dress. I'm not proud of the look, but it was a last-minute, desperate attempt to disguise myself from the paparazzi. As it turns out, instead of being on the down-low, I'm sparkling in the evening sun. I didn't notice when I bought it in such a rush, but my CANNES baseball cap has multicolored sequins on it. The green skirt fans out like two tail fins at the back. I'm a cartoon codfish, in heels.

"As if I had many options!" I call ahead to him as I waddle my way forward.

"The leggings and t-shirt you wore earlier would have done fine. You just couldn't resist trying on the gown," he retorts.

"Oh, I see how it is." I'm trying to keep up with him and feeling quite breathless. "You play it all cute and chivalrous, but you actually have a cruel side!" I move to the cobblestone path Hank's just directed me to walk on. Great. Cobblestone in high heels. We are never, ever getting out of here!

"Hey, you got me into this mess, missy!" Hank looks over his shoulder and lowers his voice. "Uh-oh. Here comes trouble."

"Trouble?" I call, slightly breathless.

"Three paparazzi, on foot, about two blocks behind us. Grab my hand, I'll pull you along!"

I take his hand, but it's no use. Now I'm waddling one step forward but pulling Hank three steps backwards. I yank off my heels and throw them in my tote.

"Let's try again." I waddle once more, encouraged that I can finally see the top of a white ferryboat at the dock. He stops, turns, exasperated, and scoops me up in his brawny arms. Then he begins sprinting forward onto the ferry dock.

"Sorry," he says. "It's easier like this. Your Tripp can punch me out later if he wants to. I'm just keeping you safe."

"No, no, it's all good," I say breathlessly, feeling both surprised and amused. "You two are going to be friends. I just know it."

"We will be, if we aren't mauled by the paps or… or by… by… now who the hell are these muppets?"

Hank puts one hand on my cap and pulls me in tighter to his chest as he attempts to make his way through a crowd of angry people lining the dock. They're shouting slogans I can't quite make out as they spill out onto the walk-on ferry ramp. Each one is carrying a makeshift wood and construction paper sign:

THIS AVIARY IS FOR THE BIRDS!
PROTECT OUR FORESTS!
DON'T FENCE IN OUR FEATHERED FRIENDS!

My eyes are wide, my mouth gaping open, and two paparazzi on the dock just snapped a close-up of me.

I don't care about bad press. I'm concerned about Tripp's safety and well-being. This is one infuriated mob! How did they find out about Tripp's plans and organize such a large protest so quickly? I count at least twenty of them, and I remember that the ferry allows twenty-five walk-on passengers. More may be coming. I look around anxiously as Hank finds a safe little corner for us. He places me down on a wooden bench and gives my sequined cap an affectionate pull over my eyes.

"You okay?" he asks, raising his voice so I can hear him above people chanting:

"For the birds! For the birds! For the birds!"

I look up at him. "A little shaken, but otherwise fine. Is there no security here?" I ask.

Hank glances around the small ferryboat, and motions with his head to the one man at the ferry's edge, lifting anchor. "There's the captain and that guy." He raises a questioning eyebrow.

"Yeah, he's a jack of all trades—I remember that he drove my taxi to the house when I arrived. So, great. No security. What if this protest grows rowdier than this?" I have to shout over the raucous chanting.

"I don't know. I'll notify the police, but it's a small island. They'll only be able to send one or two officers to meet us at the other end." He takes his phone and starts keying in a number.

"I'm glad you're here, Hank." As I say it, he purposefully moves in front of me, just in time to avoid my nose from colliding with the back of someone's sign. I zip up my blue slicker and pull my cap farther down over my eyes. Thankfully, the paparazzi were left behind on the dock, but the last thing I want is anyone else recognizing me.

I'm not just a cartoon codfish, now I'm a wet one. Hank wasn't able to get us upstairs to the covered, glassed-in part of the ferry. There are eight cars at the ferry's center, so the walk-ons get whatever space remains. I'm in a shower of sea water by the open railing. I wrap my arms around myself and lower my face to avoid getting sprayed any more. Normally, I'd laugh at this situation, wipe my cheeks dry, and look to the gorgeous orange and red sunset as a positive sign, but this protest is a shock to me. It could ruin everything Tripp has been working for. I need to find out where these people got their information.

"Uh, excuse me." I stand up and tug gently on a woman's sleeve. She's also wearing a rain slicker in thirty-degree Celsius weather. Hers is red. Perhaps she's a little kooky, like me. Maybe she just hates getting splashed by the sea water, too. If we're similar, maybe she'll be receptive to my questions.

"Yes?" The woman has long, straight, jet black hair, peace-sign covered overalls under her slicker, and dark John Lennon style shades. She's holding a CUT A TREE, KILL A LIFE! sign in her left hand. I smile at her.

"How did you hear about the island aviary project? They haven't even begun building it yet?" I try not to yell, but there's still lots of chanting going on. I hope I don't sound too defensive.

She looks me up and down before responding. "It was in the newspaper this morning. I'm not sure who's behind it, but the 'unnamed source' got their information from a government division called Island Planning. The paper printed recent records. This guy Tripp Wilson has filed for environmental protection, and that means he's up to no good!"

"Does it really? How do you know that? If he's trying to get a forest protected, maybe he's doing everything right," I argue.

"Oh, that's what they want you to think." A man steps into our conversation and puts his arm around the woman's waist. The first thing I notice about him is that he's rather hairy. He's got curly chestnut hair, a long, full beard, and kind eyes. He extends his hand to me.

"I'm Sandy. This is my wife Nadia." He smiles, and she nods at me politely. "You want to join our protest?"

"Your protest?" I ask, surprised I've met the leaders already.

"Oh, no, we didn't start it. We joined in. We're from Withybrook, England. We were camping on the beach in Cannes when we read the newspaper piece. It got our interest."

"We're minimalists," Nadia says. "We live in a tiny house on a lavender farm."

"Ah, I see." I smile, biting my cheek. She'd probably think stringing up our balcony with white lights was just a wee bit excessive. How do I win over someone who's so different from me?

"We're also environmentalists. We felt compelled to join in the protest."

"But you don't even know what you're protesting!" I raise my voice. I can't help it.

"An aviary in an old-growth forest? It won't be good for anyone but the guy making a profit on it," Sandy says, leaning back and stretching his arms across the railing. I can see the island behind him. We're nearly there. I have to find a way to stop them.

"You don't know that guy," I say, pleading with them with my voice, my eyes. "He's an ornithologist, and a good one. He isn't cutting down any trees. He's protecting that forest and the rare birds in it for the first time ever, and he's creating an open aviary where we can observe those birds, safely, in their natural habitat."

"He's not taking down trees?" Sandy asks. His brows furrow in concern.

"No, it's going in an open field beside a road that's already there. He's building on what's already been touched and protecting the rest. It's going to be educational, and it's not for profit."

"Bloody hell." Nadia looks around at the mob of angry people, shaking their signs. "How come the article stated that he was looking to make money?"

"Because it was probably sent to the paper by someone looking for revenge. This is directed at me. It really has nothing to do with the environment." I can think of three possible culprits: Joyce, Jill and Doug. All of them want to make my life miserable. All of them want me running back to Hollywood, spilling my horror story to their cameras.

"I'm Hannah Storm," I say. "Tripp Wilson is my… boyfriend. And he's a great guy. I promise. I'll take you to meet him. He'll explain everything."

They give me a clueless look as I say my name, and I can tell that they don't know who I am. This is so refreshing. I could get used to this.

"Baby?" Nadia turns to Sandy and kisses his cheek. "Baby, I have one of my good feelings about Hannah. We need to help her turn this protest around!"

Sandy looks at me, then glances at his wife. He takes her sign and puts it with his, face down on the bench. "Okay, baby, whatever you want," he says, and he takes Nadia in his arms and kisses her hard on the lips. He looks like he's going to make love to her then and there. Nadia doesn't resist. She leans into him more. Normally, I'd want to vomit, seeing a couple making out so casually in public like this, but something about this pair is enchanting. Magical. Kinda kinky. I really like them.

As they continue embracing, Hank walks over to us, finishing up his phone call. He slips his phone in his back pocket, looks at the kissing couple, and shrugs his shoulders.

"Saving trees—a real turn on to some, I suppose. All that wood," he says, and I laugh out loud. People are still chanting "For the birds!" as they line up in preparation to leave the ferry. Hank points to the dock, where I see a white cop car and a male and female officer standing beside it.

"Hannah, it's considered a peaceful protest at this point, so we can't shut it down." As Hank says it, my heart sinks for Tripp.

"But," Hank continues, "when I told them about the paparazzi following us, they said they'll escort us anywhere you want to go."

"I just need to see Tripp," I say.

The text I just received from Tripp makes my full, hopeful heart deflate once again.

<Won't be there.>

Won't be there? He's referring to my text about returning to The Lighthouse. He won't be there?

I'm bordering on tears now, and I can't breathe. I text him back:

<What do you mean? I'm here! Where have you gone?>

I lean back in the parked cop car, squished between a chatty Nadia and Sandy, with Hank pushed up against the window at the far left side. I'm doing my best not to hyperventilate. I've taken off my cap, and my hair is a netted, wet mess.

"You should put these on. You could cut your foot on broken glass," the kind officer says, and she turns around and hands me a pair of purple wellies.

"Don't look so worried! They aren't from a crime scene. We often keep lost and found items in the trunk to cover up our... uh... indecent exposure cases."

I laugh out loud, shaking my head as I take the wellies from her hands. Perfect. I couldn't feel any sexier. I'm a wet blue codfish, wearing some naked man's rainboots.

I slip on the wellies, which feel too big but will have to do, then close my eyes and imagine I'm with Tripp relaxing on our balcony, sipping Earl Grey tea. The image helps calm me until someone starts banging furiously on the top of the police car. Now I can hear others joining in, and the loud chanting begins again.

"Save the trees! Save the trees!"

"Don't engage," the female officer up front says to her partner who is driving. "Just pull away. I'll send for back up."

She'll send for back up. Huh. I wish life were that easy. I wish I could have just "sent for back up" when I read those divorce papers on my freaking birthday, when Doug fooled me into coming to Cannes, when Jill announced so callously that she and my husband "didn't mean" to have an affair.

You can't snap your fingers and have angels appear. Now that I think about it, though, Tripp, Béa, Hank, Nadia, and Sandy have all appeared like earth angels to me in my time of need. I sit back and try to relax my neck and shoulders as the cop car pulls away from the chanting crowd. I think of my true friends and find myself return to calm, steady breathing again.

The road trip that is life never goes as planned, and there are always bumps and break downs along the way. Maybe, though, if you live your life with curiosity and an open heart, someone will pull up alongside to offer you a lift, like a jump start to the soul.

Thirty-seven

tripp

<Camping. Saw the Skinks! Place I took you but not as far in. Meet me there?>

I hope Hannah gets this text; our bloody wires have been crossing all day long. I tuck my phone inside my back jeans pocket, just in case she texts again, pick up the small fence pickets and paint stirr-sticks I've been working with to make rustic signs for the aviary, and continue gluing my third sign together. I'm not fond of constantly being at the beck and call of our modern gadgets, but if leaving my cell on means Hannah and I stay connected, I'm more than alright with that.

I wanted to give Hannah space, and I wanted to chase after her. I wanted both. After I scratched out the impression from Hannah's note and learned that she went to see Doug, I drove down a stretch of dirt road for a half hour in my pickup truck, trying to decide what my next move was.

I decided I would continue doing what I love most, here in this piece of old growth forest, maybe even camp out here tonight. Above all, I must try not to throw a wobbly. If I'm going to be with an imaginative, fiery, red-haired writer-woman, I'll have to get used to her unpredictable nature. I can't panic every time she runs this way or that. I need to trust her. She can do her thing; I'll do mine, and on our best days, we'll meet in the middle. Two individual flames, creating one light. I heard that in Evan and Sarah's vows last year. Bloody choked up when they said it together, I did. Then they lit a unity candle. At that point, I had to ask Mom to hand me a tissue.

After Maggie died in the subway bombing, my therapist told me that I have something called Post Traumatic Stress Disorder. I hate labels, so I certainly didn't want one given to me, and I never told a soul about the diagnosis. But I worried when my mom didn't call exactly when she said she would, or when Coffee slept in the kitchen and didn't return to my room at bedtime. If anyone went missing for an hour, I was a panicky, stressed-out mess, and I hated it. I couldn't sleep, and I rarely ate. Coming to the island was the best therapy for my anxiety. I stopped looking at clocks or following any kind of schedule. I barely know what bloody day it is now.

I told my therapist to sod off in my mind, many, many times, but I think it's time that I return his calls and tell him he's right. Maybe I do have PTSD, and maybe only now, four years later, I'm finding a way out of my anxiety. I may see him again a few times this summer, if just to work on lessening my insomnia and nightmares. Hannah will understand. She'll probably come with me.

I'd never have imagined that someone leaving me unexpectedly could work out as the best exercise for me. I let Hannah go off and speak with Doug, do whatever it was that she needed to do, and I didn't go chasing after her in a panic. I trusted she'd come home to me, just as the Skinks finally came to me this morning.

I finally dug down deep inside myself and trusted in the strength of this beautiful love. I trusted in us. After I kicked that tin full of firewood, bloody naff that I am.

"Tripp. It's finished," Marcel says, pulling his shoulders back proudly as he beams beside the large, four-story wooden bird cage he's built. I asked him to create it for Jughead and two more exotic birds I've ordered. He's been working on this project for two days, while JF has been mapping out what will become the future Learning Centre for Ornithology, Maggie's Place, with wooden stakes. The open aviary for viewing wild birds will be built beside the protected forest, but we're waiting on the go-ahead from Island Planning. Shouldn't take more than another two weeks, at most. The fellow I spoke with said that they'd send out an environmental inspector in a few days, and because I've sent detailed preliminary plans, it is quite likely she'll give us the okay and set everything in motion once she's here.

The tall wooden cage is cloaked in the orange light of the setting sun. I sigh with pure contentment, walk over to Marcel, and extend my hand. He takes it and pulls me in for a manly hug—back slap and all.

"It's perfect," I say, standing back to admire the cage once more. "A beautiful job, thank you. Thank you as well, you two." JF and Béa smile and nod but continue with their work.

"Boo-tiful," Jughead squawks from inside the roomy, green-roofed wooden hut. He's not looking at us, though. He's sitting on his rope swing, staring at the female Hahn's mini-macaw I ordered two days ago as a surprise for Hannah. In her first task as my new assistant, Béa picked Betty up for me off a small boat this morning and brought her here this afternoon. She's also helping JF with the mapping and with staining my rustic signs.

Jughead is in awe of his new roommate. In fact, he's been rather tongue tied until this moment. Marcel starts hammering the first picket-fence style rustic sign I made, "Jughead and Betty" to the top of the new cage. It looks just right, if I do say so myself.

"How much manual labor do I have to do to get a tray of tea and crumpets around here?"

Hannah's amused voice echoes across the forest. As always, I find the tone of her voice melodic. It gives me goosebumps. As she draws closer to me I see that she's wearing the strangest outfit: a sequined cap, blue slicker, and some kind of mermaid tail. I don't bother to ask. Unpredictable. I need to get used to that.

I run to meet her, but realize partway there that instead of looking romantic, I look like a bit of an ape. I'm only managing a running limp, because my ankle's still sore. Never mind, Hannah seems to be having her own problems. She's waddling over here like a duck.

When we finally reach one another, she looks at my bandaged ankle, and I look at her mermaid skirt and blueberry slicker, and we burst out laughing. I sweep her up in my arms, lifting her feet off the ground as I hug her tight.

"You got me a Betty bird?" Her eyes sparkle.

"I got you a Betty bird, yea. About that." We take our eyes off one another for a second to watch Jughead and Betty, staring at each other from opposite ends of their cage.

"I'm not one hundred percent sure, but I think he may actually prefer an Archie." I say.

Hannah covers her mouth with both her hands, trying not to snicker.

"Seriously. He hasn't even preened her," I say. "Nevertheless, we are stuck with a Betty bird for now."

"Tripp, I love your brain, but we don't have time for a lecture on the intricacies of bird sexuality right now." She giggles, but I notice she's anxiously looking over her shoulder. She turns around, taking in our ongoing projects. "Oh, I love everything." She reads the rustic sign out loud, her voice cracking a little. Hannah's House of Rare Birds…"

"I wanted you to have your very own corner," I say. "The center will be called Maggie's Place, because, you know…"

"I know," she says, taking my hand and giving it a squeeze. It's all I need. She's all I need.

"So," I say, trying to swallow back the strong emotion I'm feeling. "Purple wellies and a mermaid dress? Is that a Canadian thing?"

"Yeah." She chuckles. "What can I say, I'm a trend setter."

"Bloody love it."

"So, you're not angry?" Hannah looks up at me with tears in her eyes.

"I was livid that you went to see Doug, but I got over it. Working on surprises that I know you'll love helped change my mood. Thinking of you always does." I squeeze both her hands and add in a near-whisper, so Béa and the boys don't hear, "I hope my nightmares didn't scare you off."

"God, no Tripp." Her sad eyes tell me a story. "I should have stayed with you. Doug tricked me—told me my mother was in trouble. She's fine, but…" She turns my body away from the new cage and my tent, positioning me so that I can see the main road where I parked the truck. She looks terribly unnerved. "We're about to have a bit of a crisis."

"Crisis?" We only just got through being separated. I can't take another bloody crisis.

"In about two minutes, a mob of angry environmentalists is going to march down here and tear this place apart. They're against this project."

"Oh, is that all?" I try to joke, but all I can think about is how dull my life was pre-Hannah. I notice three uniformed officers walking briskly toward us, followed by a muscular young fellow dressed in black and a couple of modern day hippies.

"Not them—they're on our side," Hannah explains. "These are my new friends, Hank, Sandy, and Nadia." She pulls off her blue slicker and tosses it to the ground, hoists her green strapless dress so everything's properly covered, raises her fists, and braces her entire body in preparation for a fight.

"Does it have to go down like this?" I ask feebly, and then I hear shouting. Angry shouting. The officers take their positions, forming a barrier between Hannah, me and my team, her friends, and the coming protestors.

Looking around, I grab the piece of four-by-four lying beside the cage, just in case.

"Can't I just try serving them tea and crumpets?" I whimper.

"Save the trees! Save the trees!"

Twenty or so protestors have been standing shoulder to shoulder, facing us, chanting this slogan for the last five minutes. I made sure Hannah and my team were safely behind the row of officers, and eventually, we all sat down in a circle. The protestors are still standing, still screaming. They're bloody persistent, and I have a blasted headache.

"But I'm not killing any trees." I look over quizzically at Hannah, and she shrugs her shoulders.

"Fake news, spiraling out of control," she shouts over the boisterous protestors.

I blink in disbelief. I dealt with this kind of nonsense during Maggie's class action suit, and now it's happening all over again. Can't a man be left alone to do something good?

"Back off! Give them space!" The female officer finally shouts at the angry crowd.

A male officer with a strong French accent pushes the crowd back. "You can protest but you can't touch them, or you'll be arrested!"

Sandy and Nadia are whispering to one another. She nods at him, and he gets up. The male officer approaches him, and Sandy says something to him that I can't hear. The officer raises his arm with authority and manages to get the protestors' attention.

"Listen up. Ecoutez! This one has something to say."

The crowd's shouts fade to a dull murmur.

"I'm Sandy. I joined this protest while on holiday, believing I was fighting to save this old forest, but it turns out, Tripp Wilson is doing the very same thing. He's not the enemy, here. He's filed to get the forest protected status, and he's building a center that will enlighten and educate. I hate to say it, but we were wrong about everything."

The crowd boos at him. They aren't convinced. Nadia stands, brushes some dirt and old leaves off her coveralls, and takes Sandy's hand. They stand side by side as Nadia speaks.

"Please, please listen." Her voice and stance seem to have an instant calming effect on the crowd. "Look around. Have any trees been cut yet? No. This man is true to his word. I've spoken with him about it and heard him out and think we were given very wrong information about what's going on here. You all need to hear his story and decide for yourselves. Tripp?"

She looks down at me and stretches out her hand, urging me to get up and speak. I look at Hannah. She nods. I look over at the wooden stakes that JF and Béa just placed in the ground, marking the beginnings of something beautiful, and I know that I have to fight for it. I stand up and face the crowd.

"Hi. I'm Tripp." I look out at their faces. They finally look receptive. I have a couple of hippies to thank for that. Life certainly is full of surprises.

"I want to tell you about someone." I take a deep breath, trying to stop my voice from shaking. "I want to tell you about the woman I'm naming this center after. She was good to the core, and I promise you this place will only do good."

I finally let myself exhale, and I tell them my story.

"Her name was Maggie."

Thirty-eight

tripp

There are only three protestors left in the forest. They're harmlessly standing by the new cage, watching Béa talk to Jughead and Betty. Béa is putting on quite an entertaining show for the onlookers, and it reinforces my decision to ask her to work here fulltime. Besides, that way, Hannah and I can keep an eye out for her.

I've come a long way from four years ago. I just poured my heart out to a crowd of strangers in an old growth forest. I told them all about Maggie and how I'm using the funds to build something that will do good, for the birds, the forest, and this community. After a moment of silence that had my stomach in knots, I heard thunderous applause, and the protestors started talking to one another and to my team behind me. After a while, they simply picked up their signs and walked back to the ferry or their island homes. One senior protestor did come up and speak with me afterwards. He looked at the ground, unable to meet my eyes.

"What you've been through… I can hardly believe it… I just can't imagine," he said, shaking my hand. "I look forward to seeing what you do here."

After my initial shock over what had just occurred waned, I approached two of the officers with Hannah, and they took down our witness report about the incident. They'll do a full investigation on that news article which slandered my name. Hannah's female officer friend promised someone with a badge would make an appearance at the Festival's VIP after-party tonight to pull Doug and his publicist aside for questioning. Hannah feels vindicated that at the very least, they'll be embarrassed in front of their industry peers.

Now that the crowd has dispersed, and the police have left, it's my peaceful forest again.

The sun sits low in the sky, and a multitude of birds have returned to sing farewell to the day. In the distance, I hear the Skinks Babbler, but I can't see where she's hiding in this low light. I point her joyful song out to Hannah.

"Listen. That twill-twill-twill sound? It's her."

"Her? That's wonderful. She might have babies then?"

"Anything's possible." I wrap my arm around Hannah's waist and look up to the sky, streaked with a thin veil of orange and red clouds. "I snapped a few photos before she flew away. I can't wait to examine them more closely and report to Oxford on my findings."

"Do you think we could maybe… uh… eat something before you do all that?" Hannah says, giving me a half-smile. She knows my workaholic ways too well already.

"Of course, of course. We could join Sandy and Nadia, they just said they're heading to the pub, and maybe Hank and Béa…"

We turn to look at the newly introduced pair. He's leaning against the tall cage and she's got her back up against a tree trunk. They're standing rather close. Béa puts her hand to her chest and throws her head back in giddy laughter. He leans in closer. He can't seem to take his eyes off of her.

"Uh," I say, grinning, "I should think they'll be making private plans tonight." Hannah winks at me. The little devil. She suspected this might happen when she asked Hank to come work for me.

"I offered him my tent tonight. I just hope he has strength left to work on my projects in the morning," I chuckle. "Love can do strange things to a man."

"It can?" Hannah smirks. "How would you know?"

"If you don't want to spend the night here in my tent, I'd behave," I say.

"It would be okay…" She pulls her hair back and starts to put it up. "If you want…"

"That roomy four poster bed would be better." I grin, stroking her forearm lightly.

"Right. Taxi!" She yells, laughing, and it echoes across the forest floor. Our friends look over at us, then go back to what they were doing, all except Nadia and Sandy.

"You guys need a cab? You know, back home, we have this awesome electric car, shame we didn't bring it…" Sandy says. I sense a discourse coming on, but I desperately want to get Hannah back to the house, so I cut him off.

"Oh no mate, it's all good, I have my truck. What about you two?"

"We want to set up camp here, if you're still fine with that." Nadia answers. "Clear skies, no rain in the forecast. We're happy to watch Jughead and Betty until you're back tomorrow morning."

I smile when she mentions rain. It's romantic to me now. It's all I knew early days with Hannah.

"Sounds good, thanks," I say and take the two small lace bags she hands me. "What's this?"

"It's lavender from our farm. You can put it under your pillows tonight. I also have some lavender tea in my bag…"

I do my best to smile politely at my quirky new friend. "Oh, no. I mean, thanks, but this is enough. This is lovely." I say. "We'll sleep like babies." Lavender tea? Eck. What dim-witted numpty thought that one up?

She gives me a wink and a pat on the arm, then turns to help Sandy, who is setting up a canvas tent beside mine. I call Coffee to follow me and head to the truck.

Hannah, having said her good nights, follows suit, taking my left hand in hers as we walk away. She finds the lavender in my hand, grabs one bag and inspects it.

"I know what you're thinking, but it's actually considered a luxury item," she says.

"Right then. Those four can live on this commune, while we sleep on lavender," I tease.

"Who said anything about sleeping?" Hannah looks up at me, desire in her eyes. I can't get us to my truck fast enough.

Thirty-nine

Tripp

Early morning sunlight casts our shadows on the wall opposite the four-poster bed. We look larger than life. I chuckle to myself. How appropriate. Last night, we were Sex Gods. We were like Eros and Aphrodite. Without the stalking your target, weakening its heart, and loosening its limbs part. Greek mythology is so bloody dark.

Right then, so maybe we were more like Molly and Sam from Ghost, or Jack and Rose from Titanic. Oh. Those were so sad! It seems all iconic couples have a tragic love story.

So then, we won't be iconic. We'll just be privately happy… and having lots of sex. We have so much chemistry together. Hannah sets my body on fire. I can't stop wanting her, needing her.

I curl up against her curves and pull the white sheet up to our necks. My pillow is blanketed by her long tresses. I breathe in strawberries and apricots with a hint of vanilla. I want to wake up like this every morning.

She stirs, then slowly turns to face me. "Morning, Numpty Gal," I whisper.

She frowns. "Hey. I was having good dreams, but the sun woke me," she says, rubbing her eyes.

"But now we have the whole day together. Early start. Up with the birds."

"I'm not a bird." She groans and puts her pillow over her face.

I laugh. "Yes, you are. Birds always find their way home. You did exactly the same."

She pulls the pillow off of her eyes and props herself up on it, squinting at me.

"You're saying I'm like a bird?" She raises her eyebrows.

"Yes." I stroke her hair. "My little bluebird. By the way, why were you wearing that blue slicker last evening? It was bloody twenty-eight degrees!"

She sits up, fluffs her pillow, and sets it against the oak headboard.

"I'm just a little fond of it, okay? I wore it out birding with you. I'm kind of fond of everything that reminds me of you, Tripp." She almost whispers the last part.

I jump out of bed.

"Where are you going? I wanted to snuggle," she says, adding, "You look yummy in those boxers."

"Tea and crumpets, of course. I'll be back."

"Are you going to do this every morning? Because you wouldn't want to spoil me."

"You're already spoiled, but it's no trouble. Besides, if I left it to you, you'd probably cock it up," I say, leaving the room before she throws something at me.

"Not true! You are such a Grumpet!"

I just love the sound of her laughter.

It's a warm morning, so we've opened the French doors, allowing more sunshine and a light breeze to waft across room. Hannah left me a white robe on the bed and is already wearing hers when I walk in with our breakfast tray of crumpets, poached eggs, and strawberries.

I put the robe on and tell her we look like the couple from the cover of Cruise World Magazine. She makes me take a selfie with her. It isn't too bad. Kind of fun, actually.

We set aside the tray and sit side by side in bed sipping our Earl Grey tea, staring out at that alluring slice of ocean in the distance. I never thought something as simple as this could bring me such pleasure. We haven't seen anything; gone anywhere. Just being in each other's company is enough.

"Sweetness. I need to tell you something. The other night, when I got so quiet about Béa…"

"It's okay, you don't have to explain."

"Yes, I think I do." I put my tea down on the bedside table. She keeps hers in her hand. She's fidgeting with the cup. "I love the idea of adopting her, or at least, telling her we've got her back. I was planning on telling you this in the forest, but, you know, angry tree huggers…" I make a comical, horrified face.

"Yeah," she laughs, "It's fine."

"We can tell her our plan tonight, but from the looks of it, she'll have Hank taking care of her now…"

She sits up a little. "You think? That fast?"

"That man couldn't take his eyes off her. He barely said goodbye to you! He was gobsmacked. Mesmerized."

"Yes, I saw that, too. Well, she is an angel. I'm glad we made dinner plans with everyone for tonight. We can find out if you're right."

"It'll be fun. We have lots to celebrate," I say, and I lean in and kiss her softly. I can still smell apricots on her skin. I want to push her back down on the bed and cover her in kisses, but she has that tea cup in her hand.

"I know. So many new adventures. I'm excited to get started on my documentary, and you'll be meeting the inspector and breaking ground next week!" She sounds giddy. I can't believe she doesn't know. I always flub things like this up, but she hasn't even noticed. I start chuckling. I can't help it.

"What?"

"You've been drinking that tea so bloody slowly. Would you hurry it up!" I chuckle, stroking my beard.

She looks at me quizzically, brings her tea cup to her lips, takes a long swig, and the lolly ring I put in there falls out onto her chest. She grabs it and screams. Literally, bloody screams. Then she puts down the tea cup, gets up with her lolly ring in hand, and starts shaking the ring to air-dry the tea off of it, while jumping up and down on the bed like a child at Christmas.

"Yes! Yes! Yes!" she shouts.

"Well that's not quite the reaction I expected, but we can run with it." I get up, take her hands in mine, and jump up and down on the bed with her. After a minute, we're laughing and gasping for air. Damn, she brings out my inner child. I didn't know I was missing this kind of joy in my life until it arrived on my doorstep.

"A candy ring! That's why my tea tasted so sweet!" She flops back down on the bed, and I join her. I can see tears welling in her eyes.

"It's not… too soon?" I ask, taking the lolly ring and sliding it on her ring finger.

She frowns, pretending to be someone who takes themselves seriously. "It would have been too soon for strawberry. Cherry is the right ring pop for us." She giggles, holding her left hand out to admire the ring.

"Ring pop? Is that what you call them?" Canadians are funny creatures.

"You don't call them ring pops?" She says, still staring at the large, red ring on her finger.

"They're ring lollies here," I say, taking her hand in mine.

"Lollies." She lets the word roll off her tongue. "Have a lick of my lolly, will you please, young lady?"

"Are you mocking me? You're mocking me!" I chuckle.

"I just find your accent so amusing!" she says.

"Ahem, don't get me going on about your 'O's'" I say.

"My 'O's? What about them?"

"Look, I'm trying to be serious. Let me do this right." I laugh. "The engagement can be as long as you want, but I want to buy you something sparkly when we can get to a proper jewelry store. Maybe in Cannes? I got this at the corner store with our groceries last night."

"Oh, really, this is fine. It's so you. I love it. I love you!"

I stare at her. I'm still buying her a diamond ring, even if she argues. She takes my breath away. I start to speak again, but I can't find the words. She leans in and kisses me, and I melt into her. Her lips taste like sweet cherries... cherry chapstick... warm cherry pie...wait a second. I pull back and look at her.

"Hannah Storm, did you lick your engagement ring?"

"Maybe just a little?" She gives me a sheepish smile.

"What am I going to do with you?" I tackle her and start tickling her armpits. She tries to wiggle free and screeches for me to stop, but her smile is wider than I've ever seen it before. She reaches over and tickles me under my left knee. I'm surprised to realize that she knows all my weak spots already. I have to let go.

She lies under me, her green eyes smiling. "See? Don't you dare start a tickle fight with me, you'll never win."

"Is that a dare?" I ask, kissing her delicious cherry lips once more.

"We have a few more weeks at The Lighthouse to learn who will vanquish," she chuckles. "but I wish we could call up James and see if he'll take this place off the Good Nights site and let us stay the whole summer instead. I adore it here." She looks wistful.

"We could," I smile, "but it would be a moot point, because I bought the place."

Hannah's eyes grow wide, then fill with tears. "You... you bought The Lighthouse? For us?"

"James has family in Florida and wants to stay there. He accepted my offer last night."

She's crying now. She's looking at her lolly ring, tears streaming down her cheeks.

"Oh no. I don't know what you're going to do next," I say, looking into her eyes. "You aren't going to jump on the bed again, are you?" I ask.

I pull her up so that she can sit and face me, then wipe her eyes dry and take her hands in mine. We're facing each other when I finally propose how I intended.

"I want to grow old with you in the house where we met."

"Oh, Tripp. This is... wow... this is even better than the ring pop!" She laughs.

I give her my best old man grumble. "Now wait a minute. That cherry lolly cost me a pretty penny."

"Oh, my goodness! We're engaged!" Hannah can't sit still and realization is setting in on her face. She looks overjoyed. "I have to call my mom! I have to tell her our news! She can come visit here, right? I mean, you like moms, right?"

"I love moms," I chuckle. "Maybe we could have a month alone first, though? I want you all to myself for as long as possible."

She takes my face and strokes the stubble on my chin, then kisses me hard, several times.

"We have dinner guests tonight," she whispers between kisses. "Remember? You said you wanted to put out the good silver and glasses. You were even going to make beef stroganoff."

"To hell with that," I mumble, kissing her neck, my hands slipping under her robe to caress her lower back, her tummy, her breasts. As she lies back, pulling me with her, I anticipate one of our best mornings ever, and an eternity of good nights.

"We'll just order pizza."

the End.

HEATHER GRACE STEWART

the ticket

Love Again Series
Volume One

Chapter One

Allie

"Ouch! *Mother fucker!*"

"Shhh! You'll scare all the patients in the waiting room!"

My OBGYN sounded ashamed as she said it, and yet, she kept on digging and scraping like a miner searching for gold. I lay back and tried to focus on the white ceiling. It had a bold blue sticker on it: Follow Me On Facebook. I moaned, but not from the pain. I heard the cold *clink clink* sound of tongs hitting a metal bowl. What did that make my vajayjay, a cobb salad?

Don't you think the patients outside should know that you're ripping my insides out? I wanted to scream at her; instead, I bit my tongue, pushed my feet further into the stirrups, and did a series of those tiny breaths I learned nearly two decades ago in Lamaze. Breathe in, then out, out, out, out. Try not to panic or it will make it hurt more. You are not going to die from a pap and an IUD replacement! Except, why is the doctor's face so grim?

Dr. Halo stared at me a moment, then back into that dark place, and then she started cursing to herself quietly. Most of what she muttered was undecipherable to me.

"Murble, murble, marshmallow brains! You forgot to tell me you had a tilted uterus! Damn! I'm using the wrong tools!"

I bolted up, but she pushed my chest, forcing me back down, ripping my skimpy paper gown up the backside in the meantime. "Not yet," she said, and I felt a painful pinch.

"There! Isn't it beautiful?"

She was dangling the T-coil in front of my face with an inane grin on her face. I looked around for cameras. This had to be some prank show. It had to be. Jimmy Kimmel was going to walk through those doors laughing, tell me to get some clothes on, and offer me a luxury weekend at a resort in Maui, just for being a good sport.

It had been my idea to get an IUD after the birth of our second daughter. A vasectomy felt so permanent in the beginning and neither of us wanted it, despite that Dan had told me numerous times he didn't want any more kids. In the end, he never had the surgery because he never got around to it. As I laid there in agony, having one IUD removed and another inserted, I wondered, why bother? It wasn't like we were having sex anymore. Things dried up for us in the bedroom years ago. I was just trying to be responsible, and you're supposed to replace it every five years. Still, it was weird when I found that condom in Dan's suitcase this morning. He swore it was an ongoing prank between him and Brian, his longtime boss, but did men over 40 seriously still play frat school jokes like that?

"One condom. Allie, come on, what am I going to do with one condom? If I were cheating on you, I'd buy boxes."

"Thanks, that's consoling." I tried to chuckle and brush the whole thing off by offering to make him pancakes. I felt like a royal bitch for not trusting him.

"Never mind about the pancakes—I have to get to work early."

"But you just got back from LA."

"Tax time. You know how busy it gets. See you at counseling."

We'd been going to see our marriage counselor Lori for almost a year, but clearly, it hadn't done much for our marriage. I still had trust issues, and Dan wasn't even kissing me goodbye as he raced out the door.

"Yup. She said she had a full morning, but could see us at six. I'll put the girls' meals in the fridge, and they can just heat it up. Maybe we can grab a bite after," I said.

"Maybe. Bye."

Getting Dan to go to counseling had been like pulling teeth, but after a few weeks, he seemed more comfortable and was really opening up in our sessions. The three of us were even laughing together.

"Okay, get dressed." A low female voice startled me out from my deep thoughts, and my dreams of Jimmy Kimmel sweeping me off my feet and onto a tropical island were shattered. "I'll see you in six months, unless you hear from us earlier."

Once I'd dressed and set my next appointment, I sat in the car a few minutes, massaging my lower abdomen and feeling badly about how I'd treated Dan. He'd just come home last night, and we'd already bickered twice. Dr. Halo's office is right around the corner from where Dan works. I decided to swing by and drop off a mocha Frappuccino, his favorite. Dr. Lori said it's the little things that can bring the spark back into a marriage. I had to try harder. Maybe then Dan would try, too.

Dan's large accounting firm had one main receptionist, Stacey, in a building of sixteen offices. We'd bonded over everything from our children having chicken pox, to their first dates and proms. She was very sweet. This morning she was applying mascara when I rushed past her desk, a mocha Frapp in my hand. I'd already inhaled mine, with extra whipped cream and a couple Advil, and was feeling much better.

"Oh sweetie, he has someone in there..." Stacey stood up.

"It's okay, I'll just give him this and be on my way."

I opened his door. There was already a mocha Frapp on his desk...

... Along with a woman in a short skirt that was hiked up to her hips. She sat motionless, her backside to me. His hands were on her hips; his groin had been pushing against hers. When his eyes met mine, he pulled away from the woman.

"Allie. Allie, it's not what you think." He was as white as the boxers peeking out of his open fly.

The woman jumped off the desk, then slowly turned toward me. I gasped and dropped Dan's Frappuccino all over the carpet.

Lori.

"Your mouth was on our marriage counselor's mouth. Are you giving her CPR with your fly undone?"

"Allie. It's been over a while. You know that." He wiped bright pink lipstick from his mouth and looked at me, shame and tears in his eyes.

"It wasn't over! I brought you a fucking Frappuccino! It wasn't over!"

I raced out of the room, determined not to let them see me cry.

Chapter Two

Allie

One Year Later

"Ouch! *Mother fu…*"

I'm about to scream a string of profanities, but my boss, Jed Rubicon, is standing beside my desk, glaring at me, so I bite my tongue as I hop on one foot, massaging the other.

"I mean, *Mother Theresa*!" I wince and force a smile.

Jed gives me a funny look.

My foot is throbbing. I was in such a hurry to get to my office, I didn't notice someone had placed a pile of folders and papers to recycle on the floor just outside the door. I managed to gracefully step over them, but then tripped at the last minute, hitting my foot on the corner of the filing cabinet. Smooth. So embarrassing. Jed witnessed the entire fiasco.

"You're late again, Allie." Jed frowns at me, his silver-haired brows furrowing. He's a name partner at Rubicon, March & Morgan.

"I know, and I'm sorry. The subway was delayed," I say, knowing full well that's not a good enough excuse when you're female and working for the most senior partner in one of the top law firms of the city. My commute from our home in Briarwood has been the same for five years: take the F from Briarwood-Van Wyck one stop, then transfer to the E train at Union Turnpike. The subway ride is 30 minutes when there is no train traffic or other delays, but this morning I hit 'snooze' twice, and there was no Dan to shake me awake. I haven't been able to get my shit together since the divorce.

I place my laptop case on my chair and pull out a folder. Please let this help the situation. Please.

"I was poring over these last night, and I think it might help us with the Dalton v. Steiner renewable energy appeal?"

Jed opens the file and silently reads the section I've highlighted on the top two pages. "This is excellent work. Excellent, Allie. I'll show these to Don. We'd like you to work on this case with Joan. Try not to be late again, okay?" he says as he leaves, not bothering to close my office door behind him.

I was holding my breath the whole time Jed was speaking. I release a sigh of relief, then sit back in my brown leather chair, letting it swirl around so I can look out at the cityscape.

Downtown New York, on a grey Monday morning, dirty December snow piled up on the sidewalks. December snow is so much prettier that first time it falls: fluffy and full of Christmas promise. Now it's just gross brown slush that reminds me of my failed attempts to make Gram's homemade Christmas gravy look and taste like hers. Somehow, it also reminds me I haven't done any shopping yet, and Christmas is this Friday.

I don't want to think about Christmas. I'll be a single parent this time, and still not partner. I thought after seven hard-working years here they'd finally consider me, but Joan told me she didn't feel I was ready yet.

Ready? I've billed 2400 hours a year for the last decade, missed half a dozen funerals, and haven't taken a week's vacation in three years. I'm well-respected by all the other associates. Even my jerk of an ex said I was a shoe-in for partner this year. When I make gaffes like being late this morning, though, it's like I go ten steps backward—for the record, I walked in at 8:05 a.m., and I worked until 8:15 last night. I feel like Don, and especially Jed, are poised and ready to mark one more strike against me on their secret tabulated system: operation oust Allie.

I've never worked on a case with either of them. They're always making me work with the one female partner in this firm, Joan Morgan. Do they think only women can work together? I don't get it. I also don't like Joan. She's always trying to trip me up. It's like she doesn't want any other woman at this firm attaining what she's achieved. We have enough obstacles in our way in the workplace. Why can't women build each other up instead of tearing each other down?

I've noticed Joan only wants to work on the corporate cases with the big players. I know I need those kinds of cases for exposure, but the reason I went into law was to help the little guy. I want to help those wrongfully accused and people screwed by companies.

Remember that woman whose thighs were burned by McDonald's coffee in 1994? She became a joke around the world, an overused example of a frivolous lawsuit, but if you read up on the case, *Liebeck v. McDonald's Restaurants,* you learn the poor woman was 79 years old and that, in fact, her entire pelvic area was severely burned. She required skin grafting for her third-degree burns, but she couldn't afford to pay her hospital bills and felt she should also be awarded for her pain and suffering, so she sought legal help.

Some joke. The jury applied the principal of comparative negligence and found that McDonald's was 80 percent responsible for the incident. Liebeck was only 20 percent at fault. Although there was a warning on the coffee cup, the jury decided that it was neither large enough nor sufficient. They awarded Liebeck $200,000 in compensatory damages, which was then reduced by 20 percent to $160,000.

I wish I could tackle that kind of case. I want to help clients who can't afford to pay a lawyer, but Joan and Jed snap up the few pro bono cases they're required to take on. "Billables, little girl. Focus on the billables." That's Jed's daily mantra. I should sue him for calling me a little girl all the time. For fuck sake. I'm 42! The three of them are only ten years older, but they act like that puts them in an exclusive club. Once, I told Jed I didn't like him calling me that. He just laughed.

A laugh. A good, long, belly laugh. That's what I need this morning. Everything went downhill when Dan called me at 7:35 while I was running to catch the subway. I haven't smiled since.

I swear he does it on purpose. He calls when he knows I'm rushing off somewhere, in public, or with the girls so I can't call him a delusional douchebag again.

I realize name calling is highly immature, but I think I'm entitled. In fact, that's mild, considering he left me for our marriage counselor. I wish I hadn't picked up the call this morning, but it didn't have his distinctive "ASSHOLE!" ringtone my best friend Trixie bought me a few weeks after our divorce was finalized. It's hilarious, but it gathers a lot of stares from passersby if it's on its loudest setting.

"ASSHOLE CALLING! AN ASSHOLE is calling! You don't have to pick up!" a woman's voice calls from out of my coat pocket whenever it's Dan.

I know the ringtone is crude. I know not all men are assholes. Some women are assholes. But my ex is indeed an asshole, and the ringtone makes me giggle when not much else has this year, so I've kept it.

This morning, though, the ringtone didn't make me laugh. It was a *bleeep, bleeep* sound, like I'd been floating in the pool and just dropped my phone in, which I wouldn't mind doing some days. Some days, I am far too connected.

I picked up.

"Allie James," I answered, short of breath from running in two-inch heels. I wish I'd just worn my sneakers. A woman in a matching red hat and scarf glared at me; I suppose for managing to say my name while sprinting in cute shoes. I grinned in spite of her and kept on running toward my stop.

"Al, it's me. We need to talk about Christmas."

"Dan! What number are you using?"

"It's Lori's. I'm with Lori. Can't find my cell, so I used hers. Anyway—"

"Why do you have to rub it in my face at *fucking early in the morning*? Why?"

"Al, I'm not rubbing it in your face. Life just happens. I didn't plan this. You know that."

"I know one thing: she planned it. I just read about this similar case in London, where the marriage therapist was actually sued for manipulation. I could sue, you know. I should sue."

"But you won't. You're not that woman. You're too kind-hearted. Besides, she lost her license, you got the house, what more do you want?"

"Dan, if kind-hearted translates into letting you walk all over me, you're wrong. We're not going to let our girls suffer because of our mistakes. Got that?"

"Yea, well that's why I called. I wanted to see if the girls can join me and Lori and Mandy at her parent's cabin upstate over Christmas. Maybe for a week, so you can still celebrate New Year's with them after? You can tell the girls Stacey and Stephanie are joining us, and it has a hot tub."

An entire week, alone. When the girls were little, I'd have put down the phone and done multiple cartwheels over it. Just getting a chance to poop on the toilet without being interrupted was rare back then. But now? Now they're 17 and 19, and when they aren't arguing over who gets the car or the shower, we have a lot of good times together. This plan would leave me all by myself over the holidays.

A few weeks ago, when we were discussing how we'd manage Christmas, they both admitted that they wanted try to forgive their father and get back to how things were a year ago. They'd avoided him and Lori for half the year and were only now starting to socialize with him on weekends. Lori's daughter, Mandy, is a year older than Emma, and the three girls have been getting along rather well, considering the circumstances.

"Lori is okay once you get to know her," our youngest, Emma, said after they returned from dinner that night at Lori and Dan's new apartment. "We did Wii dance with Stacey, and Lori had homemade pizzas for us!"

"She really does love him, Mum," Kayleigh added with a slight frown. "They just went about the whole thing wrong."

None of that was easy for me to hear. That they were enjoying Lori's cooking, but were never big fans of mine sent my emotions over the top. I excused myself and went to bawl my eyes out in our half bathroom. I'm by no means ready to forgive Dan, but if they can find forgiveness in their hearts, I'm not going to stand in their way. He's their father.

What would I do with myself with a week alone? Certainly the girls would want to spend Christmas Day with me, but a ski trip with a new friend their age would be hard for me to one-up for the holidays. I could feel my heart beating hard and fast inside my chest cavity, and it wasn't because I'd just missed my train.

"Dan, I'm late for work. We'll talk about this later. And next time, call me on your own fucking phone."

I turned off the cell, slipped it into my coat pocket, and took a firmer grip of the hand rail. The 20-something thin, blonde woman beside me with bright red lipstick looked down, as though she hadn't heard the conversation. Excellent. Being pitied by a Taylor Swift lookalike just made me feel shittier.

Find out more at http://author.to/hgstewart.

About the Author

Bestselling Amazon author, speaker, and poet, Heather Grace Stewart was born in Ottawa, ON, and currently lives near Montreal, QC with her husband, daughter, and three feline friends.

Heather wrote her first poem at age five, inspired by falling down a lot while trying to figure skate. 'At the Arena' was published in her school newsletter. From that moment on, she was hooked on writing.

Good Nights, the second book in the *Love Again Series,* is her fourth romance novel. Her third novel, *The Ticket: Love Again Series, Volume One*, was an international Kindle bestseller and is now published as an audiobook. She has five published poetry collections, a romantic comedy screenplay and a book of children's poems.

Visit her website, heathergracestewart.com, or interact with her on Twitter, her Facebook Page and/or her Instagram.

Made in the USA
Middletown, DE
24 January 2021

32248435R10135